The House on the Left Bank

The House on the Left Bank

VELDA JOHNSTON

A Novel of Suspense

DODD, MEAD & COMPANY
NEW YORK

Library of Congress Cataloging in Publication Data

Johnston, Velda.
    The house on the left bank.

    I. Title.
PZ4.J7238Hp [PS3560.0394]   813'.5'4   74–30255
ISBN 0–396–07061–2

75000213

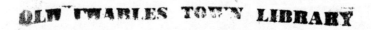

For the Schmids—
Ginny, Fred, Cathy, and Scott

The House on the Left Bank

Chapter 1

Often in dreams I flee through the night and the burning city. Sometimes before I reach that bridge over the river I am able to wake myself. I lie there in the dark, aware of my still-hammering heart, but feeling blessedly safe. Other times I cannot awake. Even though I know what awaits me in that half-ruined house, my dreaming self hurries helplessly toward it. I cross the dark river, move down that narrow alleyway, and then slide through the basement window into that black and silent house.

But on a warm September evening in my twentieth year, that night which still troubles my sleep lay months in the future. The city then stretched whole and splendid along both sides of the river, and my mother's fine old house on the Left Bank stood unscathed. I remember standing at her bedroom window that evening, looking down through the twilight at the mulberry tree in the cobblestoned courtyard, and at the high wooden gates beyond.

As I stood there, I had a sense, half-disdainful, half-envious, of the city preparing itself for the evening's pleasure. I thought of the waiters already at their stations in the softly lighted restaurants. I thought of the elegantly tailored men emerging from the exclusive portals of the Jockey Club, and hailing carriages to whirl them away to the evening's diversion. And I thought of the women—respectable wives as well as women like my mother—daubing fingertips into rouge pots, wielding crystal perfume stoppers, slipping over their coiffured heads the narrow, revealing gowns which, at the decree of the great dressmaker Worth, had replaced the graceful crinolines. In short, I had a sense of Paris preparing itself for what everyone seemed to agree was life's chief aim —the pursuit of pleasure.

True, France was at war. When as a child of thirteen I had left my own country, North and South still had been locked in that most tragic of conflicts, a civil war. For me the very word war conjured up that day when the telegram from Washington had arrived at our New York flat, telling my mother and me that my father—my handsome, talented, fervently adored father—had been killed by a Confederate bullet at some place called Chancellorsville.

But these Parisians, surrounded by the city walls and the ring of fortifications beyond, seemed only a little dismayed by their own war. What matter that the Prussians—those clumsy, ridiculous Prussians—had won a battle or two? In the end France would prevail, if only by the sheer gallantry and dash of her soldiers. In the meantime, why not stroll down the splendid, gas-lighted boulevards, stopping for a Pernod at a sidewalk café, and eventually dining on oysters at the Maison Dorée? Why not go to see Hortense Schneider, that actress and "grand cocotte" whose lovers, they said, had included the English Prince of Wales, in the latest comic opera by Offenbach?

Standing there in my severe brown evening dress, at the window of this house I loathed, I felt a scornful impatience with this beautiful city to which my mother had brought me seven years before. But that tincture of envy was there. What must it be like to feel so frivolous, so incorrigibly light of heart?

My mother said, in her soft South Carolina accent, "Martha, aren't you going to finish dressing?"

Reluctantly I turned around. She sat on the dressing table bench, her back turned to its ornately framed mirror. I said, "I am dressed."

"Won't you wear some jewelry? My jet necklace might look smart with that brown silk."

"I'm wearing my locket." The locket, containing my father's and my mother's miniatures, had been his gift to her. Perhaps in an effort to soothe my wild young grief, my mother had given it to me the day after that War Department telegram came. I had worn it ever since.

Anxiety clouded my mother's lovely blue eyes. "The necklace might make you look more festive. And you do need a touch of rouge, dear."

Without speaking, I returned her gaze. Those South Carolina grandparents I had never seen had been right to name her Flora. As she sat there in her clinging green silk gown, she looked like a bouquet of flowers. Eyes the blue of cornflowers, hair the yellow of daisy centers, rose geranium cheeks and lips. She was almost forty now. Her hair owed some of its sheen to her hairdresser, her cheeks and lips owed some of their color to the rouge pot, and she and I owed this house and the clothes on our

3

backs and the food we ate to her lover.

And yet there was something changelessly young, vulnerable, and even innocent about my mother. It was that quality which—despite my shame for her, despite my bitter resentment that she had brought me and herself to this alien city—it was that helpless quality which kept me loving her with an exasperated but protective love, almost as if our roles were reversed, and she was the wayward daughter and I the stern and sorrowing parent.

Her color heightened under my gaze. "It is just that you are so pale, darling. And—and your expression! Couldn't you manage to look a little less sullen?"

I raised my gaze to my reflection in the mirror with its frame of gilded cupids and lovers' knots. My father's dark hair and gray eyes, and his aquiline nose and firm jaw. She was right. I did look sullen. But that was the way I felt.

"Rouge is quite respectable," my mother persisted. "All the ladies of the court wear it. Even Empress Eugénie does, and everyone considers her an awful prude."

"Ladies!" I thought scornfully. Few French aristocrats ever appeared at the court of Louis Napoleon. Instead, the carriages which had swept into the Tuileries Palace courtyard on fete nights throughout his reign had disgorged exquisitely gowned women like the Contessa di Castiglione, who was said to have received a million francs for sharing her bed for one night with a rich Englishman. Always on the published guest list there were the names of other women of stolen or newly created titles, and of similar reputation.

And just below the glittering court was the demimonde, that half-world made up of rich men and the women upon whom they squandered fortunes. Women

4

like Hortense Schneider, and like Cora Pearl, the Englishwoman who had been born with the unfortunate name of Emma Crouch, and who was said to entertain guests in her luxurious Paris house by dancing the cancan naked on a floor strewn with orchids.

Too, there were the quiet, discreet women who, although barred from the respectable world, held themselves aloof from the Hortense Schneiders and the Cora Pearls, women like the one who sat regarding me now with guilty sorrow in her blue eyes. Flora Hathaway, daughter of southern gentlefolk, who'd had the bad judgment to elope with a disinherited young Yankee actor, and the bad luck to lose him in a war.

"Please, darling," she said. "This Marcel Ranier, the young man who is taking us to the theater tonight, is thoroughly respectable, and quite rich. His father is a business associate of Philippe's."

"I assumed that. He would not be taking us to the theater unless Philippe had arranged it." Baron Philippe Perruchot, one of the Emperor's recently created noblemen. Philippe, aide to the Emperor, and at the moment somewhere miles away from Paris with his sovereign, facing whatever fate awaited the French army.

"There is no reason why this Marcel Ranier should not marry you. All you have to do is to appear charming and—well, receptive."

So that was it. My mother had persuaded Philippe to get a husband for me. And he had selected the son of some family in his debt. Many Parisians, I realized, must be indebted to Philippe in one way or another.

He was a rich and powerful man, the Baron, and a discreet one. In the seven years he had maintained my mother in this fine old seventeenth-century house in the

5

Faubourg Saint-Germain, he had never visited it through the courtyard down there. Instead he always entered a tobacconist's shop in a building he also owned on the next street, walked through the shop's back room, and unlocked a door which he'd had workmen construct in the thick rear wall of this house. Even though all of Paris which paid attention to such matters must have known of his relationship with my mother, there was no one who could swear that they had seen Perruchot enter the American widow's house—except the tobacconist and his wife, of course, and my mother's servants. Undoubtedly they gossiped with those of their own circle. But they were not apt to talk to Parisian journalists whose stock in trade was articles about the demimonde, not when it would have meant losing the money Philippe paid them.

When I remained silent, my mother said, "Martha, don't you believe me? No matter what—what my situation is, Marcel Ranier and his family know that you have had a sheltered and respectable upbringing."

She meant the convent school near Versailles in which she had placed me within a week after we arrived in Paris. From the first I had hated the school. I, born and bred a Protestant, had felt chilled by the sharp-tongued nuns in their somber robes, and by the alien atmosphere of the underheated chapel, with its votive lights flickering over the faces of plaster saints, where I'd had to kneel several times each day. I had resented having to struggle to master the French language, although in time I had done so. Most of all I had hated those of my demure classmates who, watching me out of the corners of their eyes, would whisper to each other the latest story about Cora Pearl or some of the other "grand cocottes." Knowing that my only defense lay in seeming incomprehension, I never gave way to the impulse to cry out to these daughters of affluent business and professional men, "But my mother is not like that! She is not!"

And yet much as I had hated the school, I had stayed on there, even after my graduation. Despite her stern face, the Mother Superior must have had a sympathetic understanding of my reluctance to leave, because she had allowed me to stay on as an unpaid assistant to the nuns who taught mathematics and French history. Then last spring, when it became apparent that war might break out, the school had closed, and the nuns and their pupils had sought the safety of Paris. With no other choice open to me, I had come to this richly furnished house on the Left Bank of the Seine.

I said, "I don't want to marry a Frenchman. I don't want to marry anyone."

"Then what will you do with your life, you foolish girl?" my mother cried. "How are you going to live? You know that I have little actual money."

That was true. Philippe provided this old mansion, and paid the servants' wages and the tradesmen's bills. But out of penury, or perhaps a fear of her attaining independence of him, he retained ownership of the house, and kept her pocket allowance small. Even the emerald earrings she wore now, and the emerald-and-diamond necklace which encircled her slender neck, were not hers to keep or to sell. Their ownership was registered to a bank in which he held a controlling interest.

"What are you going to do with your life?" she repeated.

"I don't know." Then I said with a rush, "I just know

that I won't marry just to be sure of food and clothing and a roof over my head. And I won't . . ." I broke off.

Color flamed in my mother's face and then drained away, leaving her pale under her rouge. "And you won't be like me. Oh, darling! Is that what I've done to you? Is it because you're afraid of being anything like me that you're so—so cold, and unsmiling, and wear your hair strained back like that? You could be so lovely if you tried. Is it because of me that you won't even try?"

"No," I said, although I knew that indeed she was part of the reason for the plain brown evening dress I had insisted upon, and for the lack of powder on my face. "It's that I want to be a *person* as well as a woman. I want to be something, do something."

"Do what? Oh, Martha! Don't you know it's a man's world? What chance does a woman alone have in it? If you were greatly talented, if you were a George Sand, or a Rosa Bonheur . . . But you are not. What do you want to be? A governess to someone else's children? You'd find that is the worst slavery of all. You wouldn't even dare let yourself become too fond of the children. Always there would be the chance you'd be dismissed and turned out into the street to find another post."

I said, after a moment, "Perhaps I will become a professional nurse."

Horror in the blue eyes now. "A nurse! Is that why you've been working these past weeks in that dreadful place in the slums?"

"That dreadful place" was a makeshift hospital—what the French called an ambulance—set up in a former furniture warehouse in the working class district of Belleville. Even those most optimistic about the war's final outcome realized that soon wounded soldiers might

8

be brought back to Paris. In the meantime, our particular ambulance treated the sick of Belleville, ranging from undersized children with bones malformed by rickets to elderly men and women, easy preys to disease after a lifetime of inadequate food, dirty, ill-ventiliated housing, and—far too often—the cheap alcohol through which they had sought oblivion.

The hospital was a private philanthropy of Monsieur Ferdinand Bitzius, a middle-aged Swiss financier who spent much of his time in Paris. Like that other rich foreigner, the Englishman Richard Wallace, he provided the equipment for several ambulances, and paid their staffs. Along with the other nurses, all residents of Belleville, I received five francs a day. Five francs would not buy even one meal at a moderately good restaurant. But it was as much as the average French workman received each day. Furthermore, I liked having money, however little, which I had earned.

"I didn't try to stop you from joining the ambulance," my mother said, "because I felt you thought it was the right thing to do, what with the war and all. Besides, you seemed so determined. But for you to think of spending your life at such work! The work itself must be unpleasant enough." She shuddered, and I knew she must be thinking of tasks involved in caring for those too weak to attend to their own needs—tasks to which I had steeled myself. "But it is the nurses themselves. Oh, I realize it may be different in England, because of that Florence What's-her-name—"

"Nightingale."

"Yes. Perhaps in England a few gently bred girls work as nurses. But here in France—well, I don't like to imagine the sort of women you must work with."

9

I said shortly, "They're all right." And they were. True, at first they had eyed me with distrust, this American girl who recrossed the river each night to a resplendent house on the Left Bank. But when they saw I did not shrink from any of the tasks that fell to my lot, they accepted me. Oh, they excluded me from many of their jokes by speaking in a Parisian argot which, no doubt fortunately, I could not understand. But at least I knew that they, unlike the tittering girls at the convent school, were not laughing at me.

That guilty sadness had come back into my mother's face. "Martha, I know how you've hated your life and mine these past seven years. If your father had lived . . . But he didn't. And I could not take you back to South Carolina. Not even my old home was standing."

Nor were either of my maternal grandparents alive by that time. My grandfather, commissioned a colonel in the Confederate Army, had been killed early in the war, at Antietam. On a windy night less than a week after my grandmother had received word of his death, fire had broken out in the slave quarters and spread rapidly to the main house. In the morning, her body had been found among the still-smoldering ruins.

"Perhaps they wouldn't have wanted to take us in even if they had lived," she said wistfully. "They were quite bitter about my running away like that, especially with a man of a different religion."

Even so, they could not have been more bitter than my father's father, an investment banker and a member of one of New York's few old established Catholic families. It was bad enough that William Hathaway's eldest son should have become an actor. When he chose to place his soul in jeopardy by marrying a Protestant girl, he lost every chance of reinstatement in his father's good graces, or of sharing with his younger brother and his still younger sister in his father's will. I had never seen my Grandfather Hathaway, although my father once pointed out to me a picture of him, a man with mutton-chop whiskers and the gimlet eyes of a hanging judge, in *The New York Times.*

My Grandmother Hathaway had sometimes visited our Washington Square flat, though. She was a plump little woman with the timid air of someone who had lived for nearly thirty years with the man whose face I had seen in the *Times.* She seemed fond of my mother and me, and not only because my father, in spite of everything, remained the favorite of her three children. Twice she brought her youngest child, Laura, with her. Even though Laura was only six years older than I, she appeared to be almost a grown-up young lady in my childish eyes.

"If I had known your Grandfather Hathaway was going to die two years after we left New York—well, maybe we never would have left. But I didn't know that, of course."

No, she hadn't known until Philippe ran across a notice of William Hathaway's death in one of his financial journals, and told her about it.

"And I couldn't think of any way to support us," she went on. "Why, I couldn't even be a governess."

No, not unless she had found some family willing to hire a governess who could not spell or do any but the simplest sums. My mother's genteel southern education had included china painting, needlework, and little else.

"And so, when Philippe came along . . ."

Her voice trailed off. In the silence I heard the clang

of the bell outside the courtyard gate.

My mother straightened her white shoulders. "That must be Marcel Ranier. Darling, please, please try to be pleasant to him."

I forced a smile. "I will," I said through the rattle of carriage wheels across the courtyard. After all, he and I might like each other, even though our meeting had been contrived by our elders.

Some of my mother's natural buoyancy seemed to return. "You look so much prettier when you smile, Martha." Turning back to the mirror, she smoothed her eyebrows with a fingertip. "And as for me, I may be financially independent soon. There's an excellent chance that I'll be able to insist that Philippe share quite a large sum of money with me."

I looked at her reflection with astonished alarm. How could my pretty, feather-brained mother hope to "insist" that one of the shrewdest and most penny-pinching men in Paris share a large sum of money with her?

"Mother, what are you planning?"

Lifting her chin, she smiled at me. "Never you mind, my girl. I know I'm not a bluestocking. I know you think me rather stupid. But we stupid women can sometimes be clever indeed, if someone gives us the chance."

I have never been one for premonitions. But there in that warm, luxurious room, with its fragrance of perfume and sachet and face powder, I felt a chill ripple down my spine. "Mother, please! I don't know what you're contemplating. But please don't do anything—risky. Remember we are just two women in a foreign country—"

Someone knocked. My mother said in French, "Come in."

12

The door opened. Jeanne Duchamps, the housekeeper, stood there in her neat black uniform, with every strand of her graying dark hair in place. There was a respectful smile on her face—that cold, polite, and somehow corrupt face which I had disliked ever since she came to work in this house late in the previous spring.

"Monsieur Ranier is in the salon," she said.

Chapter 2

About a quarter of an hour later, Marcel Ranier's closed carriage moved briskly along Boulevard Saint-Germain toward the river, one of a line of vehicles carrying men and women in evening dress toward the restaurants and theaters, as well as private balls and parties, on the Right Bank. Along the sidewalks, under the still-leafy trees, less festively dressed Parisians strolled past the open-air cafés. They moved through the peculiar radiance of early evening, made up of the gas lamps' glow and the lingering daylight. On their faces was an expression with which I had become familiar—the almost voluptuous pride of Parisians in their city and the delights it offered.

Inside the carriage the atmosphere was less relaxed, although the three of us did keep up a polite conversation about the balmy evening and the number of sidewalk strollers. Almost surely my mother's plans for me were doomed. When we had descended a few minutes before to the salon, with its gold brocade draperies and Louis the Fifteenth furniture, we had found waiting for us a slight, blond young man of perhaps twenty-two. He was no taller than my own height of five-feet-seven inches, and every one of those dandified inches proclaimed him to be a young boulevardier, interested in the latest tailoring, the latest English thoroughbred running at Longchamps, and the latest and most fashionable courtesan.

In the moment before he bent over my mother's hand, and then mine, he and I had exchanged a brief but appraising look. Plainly he was no more enamored of what he saw than I was. Unless I pretended to become what my mother called "receptive," and unless Philippe put great pressure on this young man's parents, I would never become Madame Ranier.

We were crossing the river now. The water in that lingering twilight gleamed like gray satin, streaked here and there by the wavering silver reflections of gas lamps. Upstream the Isle de la Cite seemed to float like some vast ship, with brooding Notre Dame as its superstructure. It was one of those moments when the beauty of Paris clutches at the heart, even at my heart, homesick as it was for the sound of American voices, and horse cars clanging up Fifth Avenue, and organ grinders playing "Yankee Doodle" in Washington Square.

As we turned up the quay past the long, statue-ornamented southern arm of the Louvre, I heard a drum's rapid beat up ahead. Some company must be drilling, probably a company of National Guardsmen, since most of the army regulars had left for the front. Ever since last July 15, when France had declared what was surely the most unnecessary war in its history, every quarter of Paris had grown used to those National Guard drums beating out that rapid, pulse-stirring *rappel* from daybreak until after dark.

When we turned onto the Place du Carrousel, we saw them marching in the space between the Louvre and the

Carrousel Arch, with its triumphant bronze chariot silhouetted against the darkening sky. To judge by the Guardsmen's smart uniforms—baggy red Zouave trousers, gold-braided blue jackets, and red fezzes—they belonged to one of the more fashionable regiments. Beside them marched their chic *cantiniere*, in Zouave trousers and knee-length blue tunic, with her ceremonial canteen slung over one shoulder and a red fez set on her blond curls.

Marcel said approvingly, "They march as well as my own company." Then he frowned. "But I can't understand why the government is giving arms to the Belleville companies. They can drill without them. It is sowing dragons' teeth, letting that rabble carry arms here inside Paris. If and when they go to the front would be time enough to arm them."

"Perhaps," I said. "But it seems to me that the rabble, as you call them, are the ones most determined to win this war."

It was a phenomenon I could not understand. One would have thought that those plumbers and masons and wagon drivers, working for their miserable wages, would feel that they had the least stake in Louis Napoleon's glittering Second Empire. And yet at the declaration of war they had been the first to surge into the streets shouting, "To Berlin! To Berlin!" In some way I could not fathom, these gaunt men and women felt not only that Paris was the heart of France, but that Paris was uniquely their city.

My mother gave a nervous laugh. "You must forgive my daughter. She feels she must defend the people she is helping. She is a volunteer nurse, you see, at Monsieur Bitzius's ambulance in Belleville."

I did not dispute her version. If she thought that calling me a volunteer rather than a paid nurse made my work sound more respectable, then so be it.

"Very commendable, I'm sure," Marcel said politely. We rode in silence past the Tuileries Palace. Most of its windows were dark, and no carriages moved through the gates flanked by helmeted Imperial Guards. Evidently Empress Eugénie was giving no party tonight. We turned right on the Rue de Rivoli, and then left toward the theater, not far from the still-unfinished bulk of the Opéra.

We went inside and climbed, through the blazing light of crystal chandeliers, a flight of red-carpeted stairs. As I stepped past Marcel into the box he had reserved for us, the talk and laughter of the audience struck me like the sound of a wind-disturbed sea. Only seconds after we had taken chairs—my mother on Marcel's right and I on his left—I saw that the Empress sat in the Imperial box not thirty feet away from us, a diamond tiara glittering on her dark hair. Behind her stood a tall, graying aide in an Imperial Guardsman's uniform. Flanking her sat two middle-aged ladies in waiting. Perhaps she had chosen them as her companions tonight because she liked them. But one was tempted to think that they were here to set off her own Spanish beauty.

Once before I had seen her at the theater, but not from this short distance. Now I looked curiously at the small, regally poised head, remembering what I had heard of her love for expensive and provocatively low-cut dresses, and of her paradoxical prudery. In her case, prudery had reaped a splendid reward. From the moment that she, an obscure Spanish noblewoman, had appeared at Louis Napoleon's court, he had pursued her avidly, only to be checked at every move by a sharp "Not until we are wed, Louis!" At last, frenzied with frustration, he had put a wedding band on her finger and the Imperial crown on her pretty dark head.

Her husband had been with her the first time I had seen her at the theater. As I looked at his long, baggy-eyed face, ornamented with the kind of small beard which, because he wore it, had been dubbed an "imperial," I thought of what some boulevard wit had said about him. "He looks like a circus ringmaster who has been sacked for incompetence." But despite his shoddy court of speculators and parvenus, despite his insatiable sexual appetite—the one quality, people said, which he had inherited from his illustrious uncle, Napoleon Bonaparte—despite all that, I felt that there was good in the man. Again and again he had announced plans for improved housing for the poor and new public hospitals. If most of the appropriated money had disappeared into the pockets of speculators, it was the fault, not of his intentions, but of his judgment in choosing his associates.

And anyway, he had gone to meet his fate now, poor man. In mid-July, despite the agonizing pain of gallstones, he had left Paris to take over the leadership of his troops, his face rouged and powdered to disguise just how ill he was. Reading between the lines of the vaguely worded dispatches from the front, anyone not wedded to the idea that France was bound to prevail might gather that those troops were not doing well, Perhaps they were losing their stronghold of Sedan even now, while Louis Napoleon's wife looked out regally over this assemblage of his more prosperous subjects.

My gaze wandered along the semicircle of boxes and

then stopped, riveted. A plump little blond woman of forty-odd, in the box nearest the stage, had taken down the small opera glasses through which she had been staring at our box. With an inward shrinking I recognized her, from a newspaper photograph I had once seen, as the Baroness Perruchot. Two years earlier one of my classmates had left the newspaper, open to the society news, on my bed at school.

Beside her stood a dark-haired young man, also looking toward us. His face was a younger version of Philippe's, and a handsomer one, because it did not have that look of hard aplomb which, at least in my opinion, marred Philipp's good looks. But if in appearance he resembled his father, I could have no doubt that all his sympathies were with the little woman beside him. He gazed at my mother with a look of concentrated scorn and anger that brought hot color to my face.

Quickly I glanced at my mother. She was chatting with Marcel, apparently oblivious of those hostile stares. Even if she saw them looking at her, I realized, she might not know they were Philippe's wife and son. For one thing, she was near-sighted. For another, she of course had never met the Baroness, and perhaps had never seen a picture of her.

Unable to resist, I looked back at the Perruchots' box. The Baroness had raised the tiny binoculars again. It seemed to me that they were directed at my mother's emerald-and-diamond necklace. My sense of inward shriveling increased. Could it be that Philippe had not bought those gems specifically for my mother's use? Perhaps they were family jewels. In that case according to all the rules, both written and unwritten, they should have been adorning his wife's neck, not my mother's.

I wrenched my gaze away. Nothing had changed, I tried to tell myself. All along I had known that Philippe had a wife and son. Actually seeing them made the situation no worse.

To distract myself, I looked down at the multi-colored sea—ivory shoulders and bright gowns of the women, black broadcloth and gleaming white shirtfronts of the men—which filled the main floor. Many of them had turned in their seats, or even stood up and turned around, to gaze through opera glasses at the Empress and the occupants of the other boxes. In a row near the orchestra pit, my plump little employer Monsieur Bitzius and his plump little wife had turned to look upward. They smiled at me and I, glad to see friendly faces, smiled back and gave a slight wave of my hand.

Then again my gaze was riveted. Two rows nearer the orchestra pit, a tall, brown-haired man who appeared to be about twenty-eight stood beside his aisle seat, staring up at our box. Without being able to define why, I instantly was sure that he was an American. Perhaps it was the somewhat different cut of his formal evening clothes. Perhaps it was because his craggy face, with its strong planes of brow ridges and cheekbones and jaw, was the sort one thinks of as peculiarly American.

I could not be sure which of the three of us had so interested him. My mother? Surely she was worth looking at. And although she lived very quietly, I knew to my sorrow that she had a certain fame. But this man did not look like the sort to be fascinated by an older woman of the Paris demimonde. Such young men usually were barely out of their teens, with a puppyish eagerness to join the spendthrift rakes of the boulevards.

Was I the object of his interest, then? But why? Several

score women here were as young or almost as young as myself, and prettier, even discounting the fact that they had used cosmetics and jewelry to make themselves as attractive as possible.

Staring at strangers was not considered bad manners at the theater, but even so, his gaze was too intent. I found something disquieting in that upturned, enigmatic face. I frowned to show my displeasure, and elevated my chin. At that moment the gas lights dimmed, and the orchestra in the pit struck up an Offenbach air. The tall stranger sat down. A few moments later the footlights blazed, and the curtain rose.

The performance was a hodgepodge of songs and dances, strung on a nonsensical plot about reincarnated Romans descending upon present-day Paris. Julius Caesar, reincarnated as a National Guard commander, was intent upon seducing a pretty *cantiniere*. In hot pursuit of her errant husband was Calpurnia, now a sharp-tongued Parisian matron. And Nero was there, a fat man in the sort of white uniform worn by the Prussian Chancellor Bismarck. He reeled drunkenly about the stage, mouthing stupidities in a thick German accent. At each witty sally of the other actors at Nero-Bismarck's expense, the audience laughed and applauded. But I detected a hollow note in their laughter. Surely most of them realized that, far from being a buffoon, Bismarck had proved himself the wiliest of statesmen, maneuvering the proud and excitable French into declaring a war for which their country was not prepared, and his was.

The first of the two acts ended with the inevitable cancan, filling the stage with wildly tossing petticoats, black-stockinged legs, and jeweled garters. When the curtain came down and the lights brightened, Marcel

Ranier asked, "May I bring you ladies an ice?"

"Oh, lovely!" my mother said. "But let's all go out to the corridor for them."

"Please, Mother. It would be more pleasant to have our ices here in the box." I had observed that the Perruchot box was empty. I shrank at the thought of my mother encountering that accusing-eyed woman and her scornful son in the corridor.

"But, Martha! I like to see who is . . . Oh, dear. I've dropped my program."

Only seconds after Marcel had found the program and restored it to her, someone knocked at the door of our box. Even though I knew it was improbable, my heart leapt with the fear that it was the Baroness and her son out there, come to challenge my mother face to face. I saw Marcel glance inquiringly at her, and saw her nod with a puzzled but eager smile. Barred from the respectable world, and holding aloof from the gaudy half-world, my mother was seldom sought out by anyone, at the theater or anywhere else.

Marcel rose and opened the door. Surprised but relieved, I saw the tall, craggy-faced stranger standing there. "Marcel!" he said. "Marcel Ranier! I saw you from downstairs and couldn't resist coming up to say hello." He spoke in French, with an unmistakable American accent.

Marcel's smile was confused. "We have met, monsieur?"

"Don't you remember? One day last week, at the Jockey Club. I'm John Lowndes of the New York *Observer*. I think it was a London *Times* correspondent who introduced us, but I'm not sure."

"Oh, yes, I recall," Marcel said. I doubted that he did.

His expression, though polite, was still confused. In fact, with my relief giving way to a shadowy unease, I doubted that the American had been introduced to Marcel anywhere at all. Any one of a hundred members of the audience probably could have supplied the information that the blond young man up there in one of the boxes was Marcel Ranier, a frequenter of the Jockey Club.

John Lowndes looked expectantly at my mother and then at me. Marcel said, "Forgive me. Madame Hathaway, Mademoiselle Hathaway, may I present Monsieur Lowndes?"

The American bowed over my mother's hand, but did not kiss it. Keeping my own hands folded in my lap, I gave him an unsmiling nod. He was a little older than I had thought at first, perhaps thirty. His eyes were gray, and held a cool self-possession which, in its way, was as arrogant as the hauteur of a French aristocrat.

Marcel said, "The ladies and I were about to go out for ices."

"Let me bring them to you."

"Oh, no," my mother said brightly. "Since it was Monsieur Ranier's suggestion, he should be allowed to go. And in the meantime, please join us, Mr. Lowndes —that is, of course, unless you have friends waiting for you."

"No, I came to the theater alone."

"Then why don't you watch the rest of the performance with us?" She looked at our escort. "I am sure that Monsieur Ranier—"

"Yes, do join us." I could tell that he did not speak merely out of politeness. Plainly he was relieved by the thought that he would not have to spend the rest of the evening alone with a potential fiancée and a potential mother-in-law. "I will bring ices for all of us."

But we were not to consume those ices, because as he turned toward the door, a great shouting arose from outside the theater. All four of us left the box and, with others in the corridor, pressed close to the long windows overlooking the street. They filled the sidewalks and spilled over onto the pavements, a noisy, singing crowd with enraptured faces. They shouted of a victory, a great victory at Sedan. And at least a dozen young men and women, arms linked, chanted the battle cry of weeks before, at the war's outbreak: "To Berlin! To Berlin!"

Close beside me, John Lowndes asked, in English, "Do you believe the French have had a great victory?"

"No."

Too often some dispatch, or even rumor, had made Parisians hang the tricolor from their windows and then surge into the street, shouting of a great victory, or that the King of Prussia had become insane, or that Bismarck had committed suicide. Then a contradictory dispatch would arrive, and the Parisians would go back into their houses and take the flags from the windows.

"You seem a rather tough-minded person."

I looked at him coldly. "I have a similar impression of you."

He smiled, but made no direct answer. Looking down into the thronged street, he said, "What a country! It goes to war over a point of etiquette."

The war had begun almost that frivolously. The wily Bismarck, aware of how the proud and sensitive French would react, had released to the world press an account of a sharp diplomatic exchange between Paris and Berlin. Furious over the "Prussian insults," the French had surged into the streets, demanding that Louis Napoleon declare war.

"And yet," he went on, still looking down into the street, "you can't help feeling stirred by the spirit of these people. They are so sure that French bravery alone can meet any enemy's cold steel. And the poorer the Frenchman, the more hell-bent he is for *la glorie.*"

He turned to me. "But I don't imagine you would know much about that. Except for servants and a visiting plumber or whatnot, you probably have never met a working-class Frenchman."

"Quite the contrary. I work every day at an ambulance in Belleville."

That surprised him. Momentarily his eyes lost their assurance. "I had not known that people like you were taking up such work."

Not answering, I wondered what he meant by people like me. Just what sort of person had he expected to meet when he came to our box?

"As a matter of fact," he went on, "it occurred to me a moment ago that after the performance the four of us might drive around the city, and see how the various districts are celebrating this great victory. Perhaps we could visit Belleville, too."

"Oh, let's do that!" Until she spoke, I had not been aware that my mother and Marcel had moved close to us. "I have always wanted to see that quarter of Paris."

I wondered if the American guessed that she would have expressed equal enthusiasm for a midnight excursion to the Paris dump, as long as it would have meant keeping him in my company for an additional hour or so.

She turned and said in French, "Doesn't that sound interesting, Monsieur Ranier?"

Ever polite, he answered, "If Madame and Mademoiselle would both like to go."

During a drive, I might learn why this American had come to our box with an obviously false claim of acquaintanceship with Marcel. "I would," I said.

Chapter 3

In the semi-darkness of the carriage, I saw my mother's nostrils quiver. During my weeks at the ambulance, I had grown used to the reek of these narrow, winding streets. But I was again aware of it, a smell made up of old plaster and worm-eaten wood in the decaying houses, inadequate drains, and the pervasive sourness of cheap wine.

As in the splendid neighborhoods we had left, the inhabitants of this other Paris had taken to the street to find what diversion they could. Young men, many in National Guard uniform, strolled arm in arm with giggling young girls. Laughter and song and sometimes the sound of angry voices spilled from wineshops and cafés. Through the crowd, smiling mechanically at every lone man they encountered, moved the Belleville counterparts of the smarter *filles de joie* who prowled the Grand Boulevards. They were heavily painted women of all ages, from girls scarcely out of childhood to raddled crones, many with bedraggled plumes ornamenting their battered hats, and all with bedraggled skirts and with mesh purses dangling by a string from their thin wrists.

27

More than once we passed what seemed to me one of the saddest sights of this neighborhood—silent groups of women, many with a child by the hand, waiting near the doors of wineshops for their husbands to emerge, perhaps with a few centimes left in their pockets, perhaps with nothing at all with which to buy the next day's food.

We sat well back in the carriage, my mother and John Lowndes on the forward-facing seat, and Marcel Ranier and I opposite them. Even so, the gleam of white shirtfronts, and of my mother's necklace, must have been visible to pedestrians whenever the carriage slowed. Many of the faces which turned to us became abruptly hostile. Finally, after a drunken woman teetering on the curb had shouted, "Dirty bourgeoisie!" my mother said, "Perhaps we had better turn back."

"It's all right, Mother. They won't throw anything but words. They are used to sightseers, just as the prisoners in the Conciergerie are."

I became aware of John Lowndes' quizzical gaze. Several times since we left the theater, I had caught him looking at me like that.

A crash up ahead. Metal grinding against metal, and male voices raised in anger. With a jerk, the carriage halted. Marcel's coachman raised the trapdoor and peered down at us. "Two carts have locked wheels, monsieur."

Marcel frowned. "How long will it take for them to disentangle themselves?"

"Perhaps a few minutes. Shall I try to back into that last side street and turn around, or shall I wait?"

Marcel looked inquiringly at my mother. "If it's to be only a few minutes," she said.

The trapdoor closed. Up ahead the sounds of altercation grew louder. John Lowndes put his head out of the carriage window for a moment, and then reported, "There are cabbages in one cart, and wine barrels in the other."

For a few seconds there was silence in the carriage. Then a girl of about twenty-five, dressed in a plain dark skirt and jacket, halted on the curb and said, smiling, "Hello, John. I thought that was your head poking out."

He returned her smile. "Hello, Charlotte. What have you been up to?"

"I've been at a meeting. It lasted late." Her beautiful dark eyes looked at me. "Good evening, Mademoiselle Hathaway."

"Good evening, Mademoiselle Vinoy."

I had not liked Charlotte Vinoy the first day that she, a staff member of an ambulance in the equally depressed Menilmontant neighborhood, had come into the Belleville ambulance. Perhaps it was because she had made no pretense of liking me. She had stood there in that old warehouse now crowded with narrow beds, a beautiful girl despite the almost masculine firmness of her jaw, and looked at me with cool cynicism. I knew that someone, perhaps Monsieur Bitzius, had told her that I went home each night to a fine house maintained by my mother's lover.

But on her second visit she had stood beside the bed of a young boy. To judge from the size of his body with its rickets-bowed legs, he might have been five. To judge by his wizened face, he might have been forty. Actually he was ten. As I watched her, that dusky rose color which was part of her beauty drained from her face, and tears of rage and sorrow sprang to her eyes.

Apparently sensing my gaze, she had looked at me. In a silent second or two I must have conveyed to her that I knew the reason for her tears. We did not become friends after that—Charlotte Vinoy was far too busy to form friendships outside her own circle—but at least we were no longer hostile.

John Lowndes said, "Madame Hathaway, may I present Mademoiselle Vinoy? And this is Monsieur Ranier, Charlotte."

With an uncertain smile, my mother murmured an acknowledgment. Marcel, tight-lipped and no longer polite, nodded silently. Plainly he had heard of her. But then all of Paris had heard of her—Charlotte Vinoy, illegitimate daughter of a housemaid and the housemaid's employer, fervent anarchist, and sworn enemy of Louis Napoleon and all those middle-class families, like the Perruchots and the Raniers, who had risen to power on the Imperial coattails.

She seemed unaffected by his coldness. Looking up the street, she said, sounding amused, "I am afraid you will have a long wait. It is not just the carters arguing now. Half the street has joined in."

She looked back at John and said, in a subtly altered tone, "Shall I see you later tonight?"

"Yes."

"If you are not there, I'll wait. Well, good night, everyone." She moved away down the street.

Something in their manner made it obvious that when they met later that night, it would not be to drink wine in some café, nor to discuss politics. Was it at his lodgings that she would "wait"? Probably. But what difference did it make? And why should I feel annoyed by it?

My mother said, "Perhaps we had better . . ."

With the gold head of his stick, Marcel rapped the underside of the trapdoor. When the trapdoor opened, he said, "Back up, Henri."

Watched by bystanders openly amused by our plight, the coachman laboriously backed the carriage into an even narrower street and turned around. John Lowndes said, "I have to file a dispatch. If you would be kind enough to let me off at the *Observer* offices in the Place de la République—"

"Certainly," Marcel answered.

Once away from the narrow streets, the carriage moved rapidly along the Rue de Belleville. Probably in the hope that I would make the most of these last few minutes with the American, my mother began to tell the once-more polite and attentive Marcel a long story about an accident to her family's carriage during her South Carolina childhood.

John Lowndes said, leaning toward me slightly, "So you know Charlotte Vinoy."

"Somewhat." I paused. "You seem well acquainted with her."

Smiling, he avoided a direct reply. "I met her when I interviewed her for the *Observer.*"

Had he? Was he even a journalist? Anyone could ask to have himself let off at the *Observer* offices.

"I should like to have read your article about her. When did it appear?"

"About a month ago. A friend in the *Observer's* New York office mailed me the clipping. As a matter of fact, I think I happen to have it with me."

As he reached inside his coat for his leather case, I thought, "Happen to have it!" If there was such a newspaper article, he had brought it with him only to show it to Charlotte later tonight. Men ordinarily do not carry clippings in their evening cases.

"Ah, here it is." He handed me the rectangle of newsprint, and then struck a match and held it close to the paper. The flame lasted long enough for me to read the headline, "Charlotte Vinoy, Joan of Arc of the French Working Class," and the words, "by John Lowndes." I also saw the photograph at the head of the first of the three columns of newsprint. The picture was small, but unmistakably it was a photograph of the man opposite me.

I handed the clipping back to him. "You must be an important journalist, to have your paper print your picture."

"Not at all. The *Observer* practices what it calls personal journalism. It prints the pictures of nearly all of its contributors from time to time."

We did not speak again until, in the Place de la République, he bade each of us a good night, and then walked into an office building. A gas-illuminated sign beneath its third-story window said, "New York *Observer*."

A quarter of an hour later Madame Duchamps, cooly correct even at this late hour in her black housekeeper's dress, opened the door of my mother's house to us. "Monsieur Ranier," my mother said, "may we offer you some refreshment? A glass of wine, perhaps, or a whiskey?"

"You are very kind, madame, but I have an appointment early in the morning."

"Then thank you for a delightful evening."

"It has been my great pleasure."

He kissed my mother's hand, and then mine. When he

straightened, I said, "Good night, monsieur." With a certain tone, pleasant but final-sounding, I tried to convey a message: "You and I need not see each other again."

Evidently he understood. His face lit up with his first genuine smile of the evening. "Good night," he said, and walked briskly to his waiting carriage.

Inside the house, my mother said to Madame Duchamps, "Bar the courtyard gate and lock the front door. Then you can go to bed."

I followed my mother into the salon, where she took down a small painting of a shepherdess in the style of Fragonard and unlocked the safe behind it. As she took off her emerald earrings, she said, "You and the Ranier boy didn't get on well."

"No, we didn't."

She put the earrings in her jewel box inside the safe, and unclasped her necklace. "Perhaps it is just as well. You will never have the compliant nature you would need to be happy with a French husband."

I waited, sure where the conversation was leading. When she had placed the necklace in the jewel box, closed the safe, and restored the picture, she turned to me and said, "Now that American. So handsome in that rugged way! And he admires you. I saw how he kept looking at you."

"There is something very wrong about the American."

"Wrong? Because he is a journalist? Some of those foreign correspondents are paid quite handsomely. And perhaps he has good family connections. After all, if he has entree to the Jockey Club—"

"He did not meet Marcel Ranier at the Jockey Club."

"But, Martha! You yourself heard him say—"

"He was lying. I don't think he and Marcel had ever met before."

"Martha! Why must you be so skeptical, so—so difficult?" She brightened. "And anyway, what if he did tell a little white lie in order to get to meet you? It only proves how very much he was attracted to you."

With Charlotte Vinoy waiting for him? I said, "Oh, Mother!"

"You could be as attractive as any girl in Paris, if you wanted to be, and certainly as attractive as that dreadful anarchist." So she too had perceived the intimacy in that exchange between Charlotte and John Lowndes. "Besides, men don't marry women like her."

And fiercely dedicated women like Charlotte seldom felt inclined to marry any man.

"When we were saying good night," my mother said, "I invited Mr. Lowndes to call on us."

"I know. I heard."

"Well?"

"Let's wait and see if he does call." If he did pursue the acquaintance, I would certainly ask why he had lied to gain entry to that theater box.

A sudden thought struck me. Had my mother been the reason? That talk of hers about somehow gaining a large sum of money from Philippe. Had she involved herself in something foolish, even dangerous? Perhaps, without her being even remotely aware of it, John Lowndes was also involved.

I wanted to say, "Tell me about this money you hope to get." But when I looked at her, I knew I could not, not that night. She stood listlessly, stripped of her jewels, bare white shoulders drooping. She looked tired now, and every one of her almost forty years. The guilty sorrow in her eyes told me that she had reverted to the thought that it was my determination not to be like her which had made me "difficult." For a heart-wrenching moment I felt what it was like to be my mother, dependent upon a penurious lover who might discard her at any moment, and worried about what would happen to her and the stiff-necked child she had raised.

"Come, darling," I said. "We had better both go to bed."

At the door of my room near the head of the staircase, I kissed her good night. But when I had gone to bed, I could not sleep. I heard the tall clock in the entry hall chime two, and then three. It had been a long evening, and a disturbing one. My mother saying, "I may be financially independent soon." The Baroness Perruchot's opera glasses leveled at my mother's necklace, and the angry scorn on her son's handsome face. Charlotte Vinoy saying, "If you are not there, I will wait." And, again and again, John Lowndes's intent face, looking upward from where he stood in the theater aisle.

Thus I was still awake when, down in the salon, something struck the floor with a shattering sound.

I sat bolt upright, my heartbeats rapid. Who was down there? Not my mother. There was a weak spot in the hall flooring between the door of my room and the stairs. If she had stepped on it, I would have heard the floorboards creak. As for Madame Duchamps and her nieces, our two housemaids, there was no reason why they should have left their rooms off the basement kitchen, not at this hour of the night.

And yet it scarcely could be an intruder. The housekeeper as usual had barred the courtyard gate and locked the front door. As for the long windows on the ground floor, they were protected by iron grills, with only about an inch separating the bars.

With flooding relief, I thought, "Seraphine!" She was the housekeeper's calico cat. Because the salon was off limits to her, Seraphine, with the perversity of her kind, invaded the room at every opportunity to claw a brocade-upholstered chair or sofa, and then curl up on one of the rosewood tables.

I listened. No more sounds. Yes, it must be the cat down there. But I knew that until I made sure, I would not sleep. And I needed my sleep. Early tomorrow morning I would have to walk to Boulevard Saint-Germain, and there board the first of two omnibuses, each drawn by four horses, which would convey me to the Belleville ambulance.

Still, it would be best not to take any chances. I would descend the stairs very quietly and go no farther than the salon doorway. At the first sign of a human intruder, I would flee back upstairs to my mother's room and lock us both inside.

I got out of bed, lifted my robe from a chair back, and slipped into it. Once I was out in the corridor, I kept close to the wall, so that the weak spot in the flooring would not betray me, and then moved silently down the carpeted stairs.

In the salon doorway I halted. Dim light, cast through the long windows by the gas lamp beyond the courtyard, showed me that the painting which covered the safe hung undisturbed. About two feet from it a small table stood on the parquet floor, surrounded by the shattered remnants of the porcelain figurines—a Louis the Fourteenth courtier and his lady—which had been displayed there.

Those figurines had been favorites of my mother's. Exasperated now, I took a step into the room. "Kitty, kitty! Seraphine! I know you're in here someplace."

Movement behind me. Pain exploded in my head, and then blackness engulfed me.

Chapter 4

Night and day alternated with bewildering rapidity. I would lift heavy eyelids to find gaslight in the room. Only minutes later, it seemed to me, late morning sunlight would stream across my bed. Then the gaslight would be there again, followed almost instantly by the light of a gray or sunny day.

Faces looked down at me through that rapidly changing light. Most often it was my mother's anxious face, but sometimes it was the housekeeper's or one of the broad, almost identical faces of her nieces, Jeanette and Louise. Sometimes my mother's physician, Dr. Leclerc, was there, his thin face solemn and his eyeglasses glittering. Hands spooned broth into my mouth, and bitter medicine, and held glasses of water to my lips.

Finally I awoke to bright morning sunshine that did not give way swiftly to blackness. I saw my mother standing at the long window in a green muslin morning gown, her back turned to me. On a table beside her stood a blue Venetian glass vase filled with yellow roses.

When I called to her, she turned, face alight with joy, and hurried to me. "How do you feel, darling?"

"Weak." After a moment I added, "What day is it?"

"Tuesday, dear. Tuesday, September the ninth."

Marcel Ranier had taken us to the theater on the second. I had been lying here for a solid week.

"Does your head hurt, Martha?"

I realized then that something was different besides the blessed steadiness of the sunlight. During my brief periods of consciousness I often had been aware of pain, sometimes sharp, more often muted. Now it was gone. "No, it doesn't hurt." I raised my hand to the back of my head and felt the roughness of a gauze bandage.

"The doctor had to shave off some of your hair. But don't worry. It will grow back. And until it does, you can wear your hair in one of those figure-eight chignons to hide the spot."

"Mother, who was it that—"

"We don't know, dear. When Madame Duchamps found you at six o'clock that morning, both the front door and the courtyard gates were standing open."

"Is your jewelry—"

"It's still there, although the safe was unlocked. Evidently after he hit you, he went into a panic and ran. Darling, do you think you should talk so much? You sound very weak."

And I felt it. "Perhaps I had better sleep for a while." This time, I somehow knew, it would be normal sleep, not one of those swift plunges into blackness.

When I again awoke, I knew it was afternoon, because the sunlight no longer streamed through the window. My mother sat by the window, a book in her hand, and with the glasses no one but me ever saw her wear perched on her pretty nose. When I called to her, she laid the book and the glasses aside and moved toward me. "Better, darling?"

"Much, much better. And I'm hungry."

"We'll soon fix that." She pulled the bell rope beside my bed.

When she had brought her chair over to sit beside me, I asked, "Mother, about that safe. Are you sure you locked it after you closed it?"

"The police asked the same thing. Dear, I'm really not sure. And I know I do forget to lock it sometimes. But what does it matter? The jewelry wasn't stolen."

"And the police are sure the jewelry was what he was after?"

"Why, what else could it have been?"

A strange look, startled and wary, had appeared briefly in her eyes. But I knew if I asked her about it, she would say I'd imagined it, and I still felt too weak to argue. "Nothing, I suppose."

"Oh, darling! Why did you go down there? He might have killed you."

"I heard something break, and so I thought Seraphine was prowling around." I looked at the flowers. "Who sent those?"

"John Lowndes. He called day before yesterday, hoping we might be able to go for a drive, and sent those roses the next morning. He was terribly shocked when I told him what had happened."

Was he? Aloud I said, "How do the police think that the burglar got in?"

"Climbed over the gate, perhaps, and then picked the lock with some sort of instrument. But if that was what happened, they say, he must be very skillful. Usually there are scratches on a lock that has been picked." She glanced at the door, and then said in a low voice, "Perhaps that was why they also seemed to think that

Madame Duchamps or one of the girls might have been bribed to leave the gate unbarred and the door unlocked. They all three denied it, of course."

"Will the police come here to question me?"

"Perhaps not. The whole world has turned upside-down while you were lying here." There was a knock at the door. My mother added, rising, "I'm going to have some soup brought up. We'll have no more talk until you've eaten it."

When I had consumed the last of the soup, my mother set the bed tray on the floor. I asked, "What did you mean about the world turning—"

"Louis Napoleon has been overthrown. France is now a republic."

I asked dazedly, "Where is he? Louis Napoleon, I mean."

"He's a prisoner of the Prussians."

She told me then how he had ridden up and down among his already beaten troops, that sick man with his rouged face, seeking out the places where enemy fire was heaviest, and obviously hoping to be killed. Finally, unable to find death in battle, he had sent the King of Prussia a message of surrender.

My mother said, "When the news reached here, the city just went crazy. The rioting didn't stop even after some politicians declared a republic at the Hôtel de Ville." The Hôtel de Ville, a huge medieval building not far away on the other bank of the Seine, was the city hall of Paris. "Most of the trouble was around the Tuileries. I was glad we were on this side of the river."

The mob, she told me, had invaded the palace, smashing and looting, and chiseling the Imperial "N's" off furniture and fireplace mantels. Other mobs had indulged in that ancient French sport—hurling busts and statues of a deposed ruler in the Seine.

"And the Empress?"

"She managed to slip out a side door before the mob broke into the palace. Do you remember that American dentist, Dr. Evans, that I went to last year?" I nodded. "Well, she went to his house—heavily veiled, they say— and he smuggled her out of Paris in his carriage."

I felt an impulse toward laughter. It seemed to me ludicrous and yet appropriate that the woman who had helped preside over this shoddy empire should flee in the company of an American dentist.

"Then the Prussians haven't entered Paris yet?"

"No. And the new government has sworn to carry on the war. If they hadn't, I imagine those mobs would have broken into the Hôtel de Ville and thrown those new leaders out of the windows. And so Paris is preparing for a siege."

My impulse toward laughter died. Siege. It had an ominous sound. "What does Philippe think will happen? Or is he back here yet?"

My mother's face altered. She looked away, and then back at me. "Philippe is dead, Martha. He died at Sedan, shortly before Louis Napoleon surrendered. A powder magazine blew up, and he—he was one of those they never found." Her mouth was quivering now, and there were tears in her eyes. "Oh, Martha! That night when we were at the theater with Marcel Ranier, Philippe was already dead."

Perhaps because I had so hated her being his mistress, it had never occurred to me that she ever felt genuine tenderness for him. But obviously she had. "Mother, I'm awfully sorry."

She tried to smile. "I know you are, dear."

I lay motionless and silent. I could contemplate the rise and fall of governments in this alien land with a certain detachment. But Philippe's death, leaving us unprotected and almost penniless more than three thousand miles from our own country, was a personal disaster. Her plan, whatever it had been, to obtain a large sum of money from Philippe obviously was blasted now. But then, perhaps that was just as well. "What shall we do, Mother?"

"Do?" Again she gave me that forced-looking smile. "Why, stay here. Philippe's lawyer came to see me three days ago. He said Philippe had arranged that in the event of his death I would be allowed to live in this house for a year. My—my pocket allowance will continue. What's more, he left instructions that the lawyer was to pay Madame Duchamps' wages for a year in advance."

"And Jeanette and Louise's wages?"

"He left no instructions about that. Perhaps he forgot."

Perhaps. Or perhaps his natural penuriousness had balked at the thought of paying the housemaids' wages too. "Anything else? There'll be the food and other expenses to meet."

"No, but don't worry. I have managed to save a little money. We will get by until—"

She broke off. I thought, "Until what?" Until she managed to find another protector? Someone like Frederick Mosser, that Alsatian friend of Philippe's?

Twice in early July, Philippe had brought Mosser, a tall, blond man who walked with a limp, to this house. Both times he had seemed unable to take his eyes off my mother. During his second visit he had kept referring to

43

his limp until she finally had asked him how he had acquired it. "It was during the Italian Campaign," he said, and then, with an air of manly modesty, had recounted the military exploit that had brought him both an Imperial citation and a limp.

"Has Frederick Mosser been here?"

Color flooded her face. "Just once, to express sympathy." She added with a rush, "Oh, darling! There'll be no . . . I mean, no one will take Philippe's place. I am finished with all that. Do you believe me?"

"Yes." And I did. There was no mistaking the earnestness in her flushed face. After a moment I added, "Then you don't think we should try to go back to New York?"

"Not for a while yet. No one thinks there is any real danger. Why, foreigners are even coming to Paris. In the morning paper an estate agent was offering apartments. His advertisement said they were for English gentlemen who have come here to attend the siege."

Paris was not only incorrigibly lighthearted, I reflected. It held an irresistible attraction for those with a frivolous or adventurous streak.

"Maybe I would feel we should go to New York," my mother said, "if we had any hope that your Grandmother Hathaway would welcome us. But we haven't."

No, no hope of that. Five years before, after she had learned of my Grandfather Hathaway's death, she had written to my grandmother, enclosing a picture of me in my school uniform. No doubt she had hoped that my grandmother would be pleased to know that I was in the care of nuns. But there was no reply. A few months later, thinking her letter might have gone astray, she wrote again. That letter too remained unanswered.

Nevertheless, I wanted to say, "Let's go to New

44

York!" I was young, and better-educated than most women. At the ambulance I had acquired certain nursing skills. I was sure that in New York I could find employment that would support us both. But I also knew that my mother, now well-accustomed to luxury, would not give up this house for what I could provide in New York. And I could not leave her alone here in a city threatened by siege.

"You must not worry about anything, Martha. You must get your strength back."

"Yes, and I must get back to work at the ambulance." Its two doctors and half-dozen nurses were already overburdened. If wounded soldiers started streaming back from those fortifications beyond the city walls . . .

"Monsieur Bitzius has called twice. He is eager to have you back at the ambulance, of course, but not until you are fully recovered."

I nodded and closed my eyes. Fatigue suddenly had swept over me.

"And it would do you good to take a carriage ride with John Lowndes as soon as you are strong enough."

John Lowndes. Those roses had not banished my distrust of him. But at least if he had been the one who struck me down in the darkened salon, surely he would not have risked calling attention to himself by visiting this house a few days later. Surely he would not have.

Yes, my mother and I would take that carriage ride. It was my last thought before drowsiness overcame me.

Chapter 5

Five days later, on a mid-September afternoon, John Lowndes and I rode across one of the Seine bridges in the carriage he had hired, and turned west toward the Bois de Boulogne. My mother had been supposed to come with us, but when John Lowndes arrived, she had begged off because of the sudden onset of a "splitting headache." Embarrassed as I was by her obvious match-making maneuver, I realized that taking the drive alone with him would offer certain advantages. I could question him as closely as I chose without any dismayed intervention from my mother.

But I kept delaying the start of what might be an unpleasant conversation. After all those days in my room, it was glorious to be out on this still-summery afternoon. And it was fascinating to see the Parisians preparing their stand against the Prussians. They were going about it with all their customary verve. In the vast Place de la Concorde, various National Guard units drilled under the admiring gaze of parasol-twirling ladies. Others had gathered themselves into groups to sing the "Marseillaise." "That's a fine tune," John Lowndes said, "but I'm getting pretty sick of it. Seems to me they've been singing it all hours ever since the republic was declared ten days ago."

On the broad Champs-Elysées, French families from outlying districts menaced by the Prussians streamed toward the center of the city, some on foot and carrying their possessions, others riding in carts piled high with bundles and barrels and furniture. They did not appear depressed. Rather they looked cheerful, even exhilarated, like people on their way, not just to see some theatrical extravaganza, but to play roles in it. Perhaps the Paris press was partly responsible for their confidence. All the writers, from Victor Hugo to the most obscure journalist, insisted that the war would be won quickly and easily, now that Louis Napoleon was out of the way. As for the siege, it could not last more than a few weeks. The rest of France, and indeed the rest of the world, would see to that, because a siege would not mean only that Paris was cut off from the world. The world would be shut out of Paris, and that the world would not stand for, not for very long.

The sentries at a gate in the city walls stopped us briefly, and then allowed us to move into the leafy Bois de Boulogne. Silent with astonishment, I gazed around me. For as far as I could see, cattle and sheep grazed upon the grass under the fine old trees.

"A quarter of a million sheep here in the Bois," John Lowndes said, "and forty thousand oxen."

"Then at least Paris won't starve."

"Not if the siege is over quickly. But if it lasts into the winter—"

I felt oddly chilled, as if a blast from weeks in the future had invaded the still-summery woodland. Then I said, "Where are the milk cows?"

He looked at me inquiringly.

"The milk cows," I repeated. "Meat is fine for adults. But young children need milk." I thought of Belleville's children, already sickly and undersized from lack of proper food.

"Perhaps the government is keeping milk cows in the Bois de Vincennes."

Two open carriages whirled past, filled with excited-looking young women in white and pastel-colored afternoon dresses. "On their way to the fort at Mont Valerien," John Lowndes said. That was the strongest of the forts which ringed Paris a few miles beyond the city walls. "Among the ladies that's the latest rage, driving out to see the fortifications." He grinned. "And to be admired by the officers."

"They're—they're so frivolous!" I cried.

"Oh, I don't know. Remember the Battle of Bull Run? All those Washington ladies driving out with picnic baskets to watch the Union Army lick the Johnny Rebs?"

I did. And I remembered my mother and father talking of how, when the Union line broke, those ladies had come flying back to Washington, leaving their picnic hampers and parasols to be trampled by the on-charging Confederates. The memory of that conversation in our New York flat stirred an old grief. That was the last time the three of us had been together. The next day my father, already drafted into the Union Army, had gone off to report for duty.

The carriage turned around. I was silent, nerving myself to ask a few pointed questions. But before I could frame them, he began to question me. "Have the police found out anything more about who struck you over the head?"

48

"Apparently not." I doubted that the police had given the case much attention. With Prussians advancing to encircle Paris, the police scarcely could be expected to concern themselves deeply with an incident that had involved the loss of neither life nor property.

"And you didn't catch even a glimpse of your attacker?"

"No." I paused. "I just had a general impression that it was a man." And if he had scaled that courtyard wall, he must have been a young and active man, or an especially vigorous woman.

He was silent for a moment, and then asked. "Your mother is a widow, isn't she?"

"Yes." If we were to discuss my mother, better to do so without any foolish pretenses. Even if he had not known when he invaded our theater box that my mother was Philippe's mistress, surely he had managed to find that out in the days since.

I said, "She's completely alone now, except for me. Baron Perruchot was killed at Sedan."

"I know. It was in the newspapers." At least he had the good taste not to express sympathy. After a moment he asked, "But you and your mother are staying on in Paris?"

"Yes." I explained Philippe's provision about the house and Madame Duchamps' wages.

He was silent for a moment and then said, "Forgive me if this is an impertinence, but your mother doesn't seem—"

"Like a typical demimondaine? She is not. If my father had not died, she would have lived happily as a wife and mother. But it seems to her a natural law of the universe that a woman should be cared for by some man, first her father, then her husband, and then, if she is widowed and poor, and no other man offers to marry her . . ."

My voice trailed off. After a moment he asked, "Did she meet Perruchot in New York?"

"Yes. Louis Napoleon had sent him there on some kind of trade mission, about a year after my father's death. He attended an opening night backstage party at a theater where my father often had acted. My mother went to the party too."

I remembered how excited she had been when the invitation arrived, and how grateful that the woman star of the play had remembered Charles Hathaway's widow, and how pleased at the prospect of a break in our bleak daily existence. And it had been bleak. The small pension the government had promised war widows had not yet begun to arrive. Because some Washington clerk had mislaid my father's service record, it might never arrive. For nearly a year we had lived off my father's small and ever-diminishing life insurance. I could remember sharing her excitement as I helped her refurbish her lavender silk evening gown.

That night, eager to hear about the party, I struggled to stay awake until she came home. Thus when she softly opened the door of my room, I was sleeping so lightly that I instantly awoke. "Mother, tell me about it."

She lit the oil lamp and sat down beside my bed. How lovely she looked with her flushed face, and in the low-cut gown that was such a contrast to the black mourning garments she had worn whenever she stirred outside our flat that past year.

"Darling, it was wonderful! And—oh, Martha! How would you like to go to Paris?"

50

I said, bewildered, "Paris, France?"

"Yes, darling. I met a Frenchman tonight. A baron! He is sure that a Paris theatrical producer he knows will send me a contract."

Her gaze had slid away from mine. "But, Mother! You're not an actress."

"You don't understand, darling. In some comic operas you don't have to act. They pay you just to move around on the stage and look pretty."

Certainly she could do that. "But, Mother, what if we go over there, and then the theatrical producer doesn't like you?"

Her color deepened. "I will still have the contract. He will have to pay me, whether or not he gives me parts in his productions. And he will pay enough that you and I will be able to live very nicely."

I rather imagine my mother had insisted upon that particular bit of camouflage. All I am sure of is that the contract arrived within a few weeks. Several days later Grandmother Hathaway paid us one of her rare visits. Her nineteen-year-old daughter Laura—technically my Aunt Laura, although I, only six years her junior, never called her that—climbed with my grandmother the two flights to our door. The surviving Hathaway son, James, had driven with them from their house on upper Fifth Avenue, but he did not climb the stairs. Neither before nor after my father's death had he consented to meet the Protestant woman that his scapegrace brother, not content with disgracing the Hathaway name by strutting on the stage, had chosen to marry. Looking out the window. I saw him sitting down there in the open carriage. Even though he had no muttonchop whiskers, and his hair was blond rather than gray, his ramrod posture reminded me of that newspaper picture I had seen of my formidable grandfather.

My mother showed Grandmother Hathaway the contract. "Flora!" My grandmother's face was dismayed. "Surely you're not going on the stage, especially not in France." She flushed. "Yes, I know Charles was an actor." Her voice trembled over the name of her favorite child. "But it is different for a man. For a woman it is little better than . . ." She broke off, glancing at me.

"Isn't that a rather old-fashioned idea?" My mother's face, too, had grown flushed. "Besides," she went on passionately, "what do you expect me to do? Live out my life in this flat, with not even enough money to replace those gone-to-pieces window draperies? And what of Martha? In a few years she'll be grown up. She'll want pretty clothes, like any other girl."

Laura Hathaway, who seldom said much during these visits, said nothing then. But she expressed her distaste by rising, walking to the window, and standing with her back turned, as if wishing she had stayed down there in the carriage with her brother.

"It's the child I'm thinking of," my grandmother said. "She should have the proper atmosphere—"

"She'll have it." Now my mother's voice rang with confidence. "She'll go straight into a convent school."

My grandmother sighed. "I suppose I have no right to try to stop you." She glanced at her daughter's rigid back, and then went on in a low voice, "You know I would have been helping you all along if I could. But Mr. Hathaway makes me account for every penny." I had never heard her call my grandfather anything but Mr. Hathaway.

A few minutes later she rose, kissed my mother and me, and said, "Come, Laura. We must leave." It was the last time I had either seen or heard from my grand-mother and my young aunt and my not much older uncle. A week after that my mother and I had sailed for France. Baron Perruchot was aboard too, in a cabin well away from our own.

In Paris we went straight to the house in Faubourg Saint-Germain, "which friends of the Baron have been kind enough to prepare for us." A few days later, while we were getting ready to take the train to my school near Versailles, my mother told me that she was not to be an actress after all. "That theatrical man said I wouldn't do," she said blithely. "But that's all right. He had to pay me an enormous sum, enough to keep us— oh, for years."

I believed her then, and for months thereafter. Per-haps she had hoped that in that convent school I would go on believing indefinitely. She had never been away to school. She had no idea how sophisticated boarding school misses can become, exchanging whispered confi-dences in the dormitories, and, after visits home, smug-gling into the school newspapers and magazines filled with gossip.

She must have hoped, too, that my father's family, and most importantly my Grandmother Hathaway, would be deceived. But despite Philippe's care to never visit the Saint-Germain house except by that door at the rear of the tobacconist's shop, soon all Paris that concerned it-self with such matters knew the truth. And in the years since the close of the War, surely more than one ac-quaintance of the Hathaway family had visited Paris and brought back stories about Flora Hathaway. No wonder

53

my mother's letters to my grandmother had gone unanswered.

John Lowndes broke in on my thoughts. "What was your father like?"

"An actor." I smiled, remembering how proud I used to be when he strode up and down the kitchen of our flat, rehearsing the St. Crispian's speech from *Henry the Fifth*, or the role of Charles Surface in *School for Scandal*. Even better I liked the times when he amused me with a one-man minstrel show, playing both Mr. Bones and the Interlocutor, and interspersing the jokes with songs and a strutting cakewalk.

"To me he was the most charming man alive," I said. I took the locket from around my neck, snapped it open, and handed it to him. "Here is his picture, and my mother's."

We both looked down at the oval miniatures of my fair-haired mother and my dark-haired, aquiline-nosed father. How young they both looked—far too young to be parents, although I was already three weeks old the day my father gave that locket to my mother.

"He had those miniatures made from photographs," I said, "for their first anniversary."

John Lowndes studied the pictured faces, and then closed the case and turned it over. On the back were the engraved words, "From Charles Hathaway to Flora Hathaway, with eternal love."

I said, "Having that engraved must have cost him extra, and I'm sure that the miniatures alone had cost more than he could afford, but he was like that."

He handed the locket back to me. "You resemble your father very closely."

"Yes." I knew that my mother secretly wished, for my

54

own sake, that I had inherited a fragile blondness, either from her or from the blond members of the Hathaway family. But I was content to resemble my father.

We were inside the city walls now, moving along a Champs-Elysées still crowded with carriages, drilling Guardsmen, and bundle-laden new arrivals from beyond the fortifications. I had answered his questions. Now it was my turn. But still I hesitated to ask the crucial questions—perhaps because the red-gold sunlight of late afternoon lay so warmly on the sculptures in the Place de la Concorde, perhaps because it was so pleasant to ride through this splendid but alien city with a compatriot, even one who had given me reason to mistrust him.

I said, "You don't sound like a New Yorker. You're not, are you?"

"No. I grew up in a little town in Illinois."

The state Lincoln had grown up in. I was not surprised. Although John Lowndes was much younger and more handsome, he had that raw-boned, western look which Lincoln had brought with him out of Illinois, and never lost.

"I went to work on a Chicago newspaper when I was twenty-one. Later I joined the New York *Observer*. Because I spoke French, the newspaper sent me here when it became apparent war might break out."

I had wondered about his fluent French. "How is it that you speak French so well?"

"My stepmother—my own mother died when I was two—was the daughter of a French-Canadian schoolmaster. I grew up bilingual."

We were crossing the Seine, its waters opalescent in the sunset light. If I was to ask those questions, it would have to be now. "You never met Marcel Ranier at the

55

Jockey Club, did you? Until you came to our box, you had never met him anywhere."

After a moment he said, gaze fixed on the coachman's broad back. "No, I had never met him."

"Then why did you pretend you had?"

"Because I wanted to meet you, and I could think of no other way of managing it. I asked some people I knew in the audience, and they told me Ranier's name, and that he was a member of the Jockey Club."

The very calmness of his tone angered me. "Those acquaintances of yours, did they also tell you who my mother was?"

He hesitated, and then said, "Yes."

"Why did you want to meet me?"

"Because I found you attractive, of course."

I could not protest that without sounding insufferably coy. "Surely I was not the only woman there you thought attractive." Anger made my voice shake. "Or did you hope that it was a case of like mother, like daughter?"

"On the contrary." He still spoke with that irritating calm. "What attracted my attention was that plain brown dress, and your unpowdered face shining in the light, and the stiff-necked way you held your head." He chuckled. "You reminded me of a stern young vestal virgin who somehow had found herself in a crowd of nymphs, satyrs, and bacchantes."

Was he telling the truth? Perhaps. Although I was what people called inexperienced, I had read enough, and observed enough, to know that some men ignore all women except those with inviting smiles. Other men, perhaps those with more of the hunter's instinct, find aloof women an irresistible challenge.

56

Perhaps he really did find me attractive. The thought brought me a stir of emotion I had never felt before. Feeling a little frightened, I realized that it was not just my suspicion of him which had made me agree to that sight-seeing trip through Belleville, and made me welcome the chance to be alone with him today.

He asked, "Then you'll forgive my little ruse?"

I tried to sound matter-of-fact. "I suppose so."

We had turned onto the Left Bank quay. After a few moments he said, "I'll be out of Paris for a few weeks. My paper wants me to go beyond the Prussian lines to interview General Sheridan."

I nodded. I had read in the press that the American general was an observer with the Prussian army.

"When I come back, I want to do a story on all of Paris's medical facilities, including the ambulances."

"You mean you want to interview me? I'm no Joan of Arc of the working class, you know."

Instantly I regretted the remark. I had meant to sound lightly amused. Instead I had sounded waspish. He said, "No, what I was leading up to is this. Do you plan to stay with the ambulance?"

"Of course."

"I advise that you resign, right now. Taking care of ordinary sick people is one thing. But if this war goes the way I think it will—well, by Christmas you'll be wishing you were anywhere except that place."

Those other nurses at the ambulance would not quit. Certainly his Joan of Arc would not leave her ambulance. "I plan to stay."

The carriage had turned onto Boulevard Saint-Germain, with its sidewalk cafés already filled with people enjoying an early evening apértif. "Then at least join the ambulance some Americans in Paris have set up. They have the best equipment, and the administrator and some of the staff members are American."

"No, I can't leave Monsieur Bitzius's ambulance."

The Swiss financier's youngest daughter had been one of my pupils during the year following my graduation, when I had helped the nuns teach mathematics and history. At their daughter's graduation, Monsieur and Madame Bitzius had sought me out to thank me. Furthermore—and this was what had won my enduring gratitude—twice last summer they had invited my mother and me to dinner. Never before in all her years in Paris had a respectable couple like the Bitziuses invited her into their home.

John sighed and shook his head. "Back in Illinois we have a saying. 'You can never win an argument with a tornado, a balky mule, or a stubborn woman.' "

He turned to me, smiling. As I looked into his gray eyes, I felt my uneasy defensiveness slipping away. Something was unfolding in my heart—a kind of warm, tremulous wonder.

He would be back in a few weeks. And then, despite the beautiful and brilliant Charlotte, he would seek me out.

Chapter 6

Late in the afternoon ten weeks later, I moved along the aisle between the close-packed beds in the ground floor ward. The old warehouse had no windows on that floor. Consequently we had to keep the street door open day and night, despite the fact that this winter was the coldest within the memory of most Parisians. As I neared the flimsy partition that protected the patients against the worst of the December blasts, I felt the increasing iciness of the air.

In the little vestibule I leaned against one side of the doorway and looked out into the gray, wind-swept street. As happened far too often, I found myself thinking of John Lowndes—John, who apparently had not returned to the city after all. At least I had heard nothing from him since that beautiful September day when we had driven through the Bois.

By Christmas, he had said, I would be wishing I was anywhere but at the Belleville ambulance. Christmas was still almost two weeks away, and already I was wishing it.

If only for a few minutes,. I needed respite from my endless tasks—administering food and medicine, bathing fevered bodies, rebandaging wounds. Most of all I needed respite from sound and sight of the suffering that filled all three floors of the ambulance. The ground floor beds held only soldiers now, wounded survivors of early December's "great sortie," a disastrous attempt to break through the iron ring of Prussian besiegers and join up with French forces in other parts of France. Twelve thousand Frenchmen had died in that futile attempt.

To make way for the wounded, all other patients, most of them children, had been moved to the floors above. There were many more child patients now. With the thermometer hovering only a few degrees above zero, pneumonia and smallpox were claiming children who had less than ever to eat, and no milk at all.

Unbelievably, infuriatingly, the government *had* failed to bring herds of milk cows inside the fortification.

I not only felt tired and sad. I felt hungry. But then, nearly everyone was. Those cattle and sheep I had seen in the Bois that day were gone now. If you had the money, you could still buy mutton and beef from the Rue Saint-Honoré butcher shops, at ten to twenty times last September's prices. Other meat had been salted down by those with enough money and foresight to stockpile food. But most of the beef and mutton had long since disappeared down the throats of nearly two million Parisians. Horsemeat, once eaten only in such neighborhoods as this, now was sought eagerly by the middle classes. Since mid-November, butcher shops had been offering cat and dog meat. And now slaughter of the zoo animals—elephants, camels, foxes, wolves—had begun.

As I leaned there in the doorway, I longingly remembered the taste of butter. A pound of it would have cost me thirty-five francs, my wages for seven days.

60

An elderly man shuffled past through the fading light, a rolled-up newspaper under his arm. Again I was reminded of John Lowndes. No copies of the *Observer* or any other foreign journals ever got through the Prussian lines, nor did any letters. Nevertheless, thanks to carrier pigeons, letters did reach Paris from other parts of France and even other countries, by what the Parisians promptly had dubbed "pigeon post." Surely if he had wanted to, John could have used the pigeon post to write to me.

Monsieur Bitzius turned into the doorway, a hat pulled low on his bald head with its fringe of gray hair, his round face reddened by the wind. "Martha! Aren't you cold standing there?" His eyes, a bright blue behind silver-rimmed glasses, looked at me closely. "Or are you too tired to feel the cold?"

I smiled. "It's been a bad day. But tomorrow is Friday, my day off."

"This ambulance is full enough, without your getting sick. You're off duty in half an hour anyway, aren't you?" I nodded. "Well, get your cloak, walk down to Madame Lamartine's for a glass of wine, and then go home."

"Thank you, I will. I only wish it could be hot chocolate."

"They have chocolate." When I looked at him incredulously, he lowered his voice and said, "Madame Lamartine told me that the ambulance staff members can have a cup now and then. It won't be made with milk, of course."

"It will still taste wonderful."

A few minutes later, in my heavy dark blue cloak, I hurried down the street to Madame Lamartine's. A half-dozen gaunt women, one with a shawl-wrapped baby in her arms, waited silently outside the door. When I went into the dark low-ceilinged café, I understood why they waited. The café's outer room was empty, but from behind a thin partition came the sound of talk and laughter, and a voice roaring out one of the coarse ballads about the deposed Empress Eugénie. National Guardsmen back there, spending their one-and-a-half-francs' daily pay on glass after glass of wine. If the city's food supplies dwindled to one shriveled cabbage leaf, I reflected, no doubt there still would be an inexhaustible supply of wine. Madame Lamartine brought me a cup of chocolate, and I sipped it slowly, trying to make it last as long as possible.

Charlotte Vinoy appeared in the café doorway. She was thinner now, like everyone else, but her complexion still had that dusky rose glow and her dark eyes that look of indomitable pride. She walked over to my table. "May I join you?"

"Of course."

She sat down. "Is that chocolate?"

I nodded. "By courtesy of Monsieur Bitzius. I am sure he would like for you to have a cup too."

"Thank you, but I don't like chocolate." She called to Madame Lamartine, behind the counter, "A glass of red wine, please."

When her wine came, she took a sip and then asked, "How do things go at your ambulance?"

"The same as at yours, I imagine. Children too starved to get well. Men losing their legs, and then their lives."

She nodded, and then burst out, "But it needn't have been like this. The sortie could have succeeded. It's just that our damnable, weak-spined, bourgeois government

62

didn't plan properly. At the very least, they should have allowed the National Guard to take part."

Working hard and eating little, I'd had no energy or inclination to follow the intricacies of French politics. But I did know that from the moment Louis Napoleon's government toppled, there had been a bitter struggle between the moderate Republicans and the radicals. Some weeks before, the radical leaders had tried to seize power. A shouting, fist-swinging brawl at the Hôtel de Ville had ended with the moderates still in charge and several of the opposition leaders in jail.

"It's the same old story," she went on, her dark eyes furious. "It's the working people, with nothing but their lives and their love of country, who want to fight for France."

Another burst of song came from beyond the partition. "And while they are waiting to lay down their lives," I said dryly, "they spend what little they have on drink, and their women stand in food queues, and their children die."

"You don't understand! For generations the French worker has not had enough to feed his family adequately, no matter how hard he tried, or how sober he was. Can you blame them for numbing themselves with drink?"

"Yes, I still can," I wanted to say, but did not. As a citizen of ever-expanding America, with its opportunities for even the most humble, perhaps I would never appreciate the reasons for France's bitter class warfare.

She said, echoing my own thought, "But then, I couldn't you expect you to understand."

"You mean, because I am an American, and a member of what you call the bourgeoisie? But doesn't that apply to your friend John Lowndes, too?" As I said it, I realized that ever since she appeared, I had been wanting to speak his name.

"It certainly does. I told him that just the other night. He laughed and said that a journalist was just a spectator, not a member of any class."

For a moment I sat motionless and silent. "The other night? Then he's back in Paris?"

"Why, yes. He's been back since mid-November."

And he had not come near me. So much for his being "attracted" to me. I looked like "a stern young vestal virgin" among the bacchantes, he had said. Now I realized that I, daughter of Philippe Perruchot's mistress, must have appeared to him a ridiculous prude, sitting there in my plain brown dress that was like a moral judgment upon most of the women there, including my own mother. I had aroused his amused curiosity. As soon as he had satisfied it, he had no further interest in me. What a fool I had been all these weeks, hoping each morning that before the day was over I would see him.

In my pain and humiliation, I wanted to strike out at the beautiful girl across the table. "I should think you would have little time to waste on 'just a spectator.'"

"It's not wasted. Arguing with him helps me clarify my ideas. And working and attending meetings does not absorb all my energies.

"Anyway," she went on, "I don't feel that any man, any individual, should matter too much. It is the cause that counts." Her voice hardened. "And this time the cause will win. This time we have arms."

After what I had just learned about John Lowndes, I was in no mood to discuss the now-armed National Guard. All I wanted was to get away from there.

64

I said goodbye and laid a coin beside my saucer. Outside in the windy street, I turned toward the wider Rue Ramponeau, and then toward the corner where the omnibus stopped.

Perhaps it was my own mood, but as the two teams of horses drew us over the paving stones, it seemed to me that my fellow passengers looked more wan than usual, and the once-lively Paris streets more dreary. Many of the shops and cafés, with nothing to sell, had shuttered their windows. Pedestrians did not stroll, but hurried through the dusk, shoulders hunched against the cold. And doorways no longer sheltered *filles-de-joie*, smiling at each male passer-by. The police had rounded most of them up and put them to work. Some sewed National Guard uniforms. Others worked in the balloon factory set up in a vast and echoing railroad station.

Those flimsy balloons, filled with highly inflammable coal gas, were now the city's chief means of communicating with the outside world. Launched in pre-dawn darkness, they soared out over the heads of the encircling Prussians, some carrying only dispatches and letters, others with one or two brave men in the little basket beneath the wind-tossed sphere. Some balloons had been shot down by the Prussians. Some had plunged into the English Channel. But many of them landed safely beyond the enemy lines, and eventually the messages they carried had reached their destinations.

John Lowndes, I reflected, must be sending out dispatches from Paris by every balloon, confident that some of them eventually would reach New York. And then I thought bitterly, "Who cares about John Lowndes and his dispatches?"

The omnibus had stopped. Three passengers got on,

including one I recognized, an old man in a shiny black suit of outmoded cut, and a straggly gray beard. He was Jules Richard, chemist. One of Philippe's many enterprises had been a laboratory near the Gare du Nord, where Professor Richard and other chemists experimented with possible new products—from more adhesive glues to longer-lasting dyes for clothing. He saw me, shouted "Mademoiselle Hathaway!" and with surprising agility darted past a shawled woman who had been moving toward the vacant seat beside me.

He sat down, breathing hard. "Mademoiselle, I am so very glad to see you."

"And I to see you," I said untruthfully. As on the first occasion we met, his suit bore food stains, and he spluttered when he talked.

"Please tell your mother that she must allow me to see her."

I felt surprise. "You have tried to see my mother?"

"Several times, ever since I heard of the Baron's death. I did not hear of it immediately. I was ill for a time last September—very ill. But when I did hear, I went straight to your mother. That dragon of a housekeeper you have left me standing on the doorstep and then told me that Madame Hathaway was indisposed. Since then your housekeeper has refused even to announce me to your mother. Each time she says that Madame Hathaway is not at home."

I felt sure why my mother had not been at home to Professor Richard. The one time Philippe had asked him to the Saint-Germain house for dinner, he had not only displayed very bad table manners. He had talked on and on about the effect of a newly developed antiseptic upon open wounds, until my mother, greenish pale, stopped even trying to eat. At last Philippe, looking amused, had said, "Perhaps, Professor Richard, you and I had better save these topics until the ladies leave us with our brandy and cigars."

Now I said, "You must forgive my mother. She finds life a great strain these days."

That was true. We did not have the money to buy from the expensive butchers and greengrocers, where one did not have to stand in line. And so often before daylight not only Madame Duchamps and one of the maids, but my mother as well, left the house to stand in three separate food queues. At least one of the three of them always managed to buy something before the day's supplies were exhausted.

What was more, perhaps because of overstrained nerves, she had taken to lingering down in the salon, reading or doing needlework, until long after I had gone to bed. Sometimes, only half asleep, I would hear her step on that weak spot in the hall flooring on her way to her room. Other nights I had no idea at what hour she went to bed. When I remonstrated with her, she said she "made up for it" by taking long afternoon naps.

Now I said to the Professor, "If you wanted to express your sympathy over the Baron's death—"

"It is more than that. I have other matters to discuss with your mother."

What could he and my mother possibly have to discuss? I looked at the eyes glittering behind his glasses. Not for the first time, it occurred to me that the good Professor might be a little mad. "Then I will convey to her any message you like."

"You, mademoiselle? You are a child."

I said, amused, "I am twenty."

"It is as I have said. You are a child. I cannot trust anyone, particularly a person of tender years." He looked around him and then, lowering his voice, leaned close to me. "These are dangerous times, and may grow more so. A man in my situation might be shot. And I am innocent of any wrong intent—absolutely innocent."

"I am sure you are, Professor," I said, leaning as far away from him as possible. "And I will tell my mother that you would like to see her." But I certainly would not urge her to do so.

"Please do. My patience is wearing thin."

"Here is my transfer point, Professor." While the omnibus was still in motion, I slipped past his bony knees and went down the aisle.

When I finally reached the house, my mother opened the door for me. "You look so tired, darling," she said, "and so cold."

"You look tired too." She was still lovely, but her blue eyes seemed almost too large now. She had lost that rosy, rounded look which the young painter Renoir gave to his portraits of women. I said, unbuttoning my cloak, "Professor Richard was on the omnibus. He said that he has tried several times to see you."

Her lips tightened. "I will not see that dreadful old man. If he had something to say to me, he can write me a letter. How dare he keep coming here? I really believe he is mad."

"So do I."

"Let's not talk about him. Darling, something nice has happened. Someone sent you a present."

"A present?"

"John Lowndes' card is inside." My heart gave an odd little lurch. "Forgive me for opening your present. I just couldn't wait to see what he had sent. But I tied it up again, so you would have the pleasure of undoing it."

With her arm around my waist, we moved into the salon. On one of the tables rested a square package, about large enough to contain a nosegay or a lavish bottle of perfume. It was wrapped in silver paper, with a spray of artificial violets thrust through the bow of its narrow silver ribbon.

With unsteady fingers, I untied the ribbon and lifted the lid of the box. My mother and I gazed reverently at its contents.

"It must weigh almost a pound," I said.

"A little more. Madame Duchamps and I weighed it on the kitchen scale."

Tears sprang to my eyes. He had not forgotten me—at least not entirely. He had sent me a gift more precious than either flowers or perfume—a large wedge of yellow cheese.

Chapter 7

The next morning I mailed a thank-you note to the *Observer* offices. For several days thereafter I kept expecting John Lowndes to appear, either at the house or at the ambulance. He did not. What a strange man, I thought, feeling a bewildered resentment. He had sent me a gift worth more than a week of my wages, and yet apparently he had no desire to see me.

Toward the end of that week I came home one night to find my mother more pale and distraught-looking than ever. At dinner she scarcely touched the food Madame Duchamps had set before us—carrots and potatoes simmered in the broth from a soup bone. She dropped her fork and then, a few moments later, upset her water glass.

I said, as she daubed at the spreading moisture with her napkin, "Mother, what is it? Did something happen today? Did that Professor Richard come here again?"

"No, dear. No one has been here."

But certainly something weighed upon her. I had assumed that Philippe's death meant the end of her plan, whatever it had been, to obtain a large sum of money. Could I have been wrong about that? Perhaps she still

70

was enmeshed in something I knew nothing about—something that kept her keyed-up with expectation, or anxiety, or both.

"Mother, do you remember mentioning months ago that you hoped to get a large sum of money from Philippe?" I saw the startled look in her eyes. "You never explained to me what that was about."

"Darling, it was just some sort of investment plan he wanted me to help him with. I never really understood it."

"What did he want you to do?"

She said, after a moment, "Sign some sort of paper. Or maybe get someone else to sign some sort of paper. Anyway, he said that there would be quite a lot of money in it for me."

"What sort of investment was it?"

"Stocks, I think, or bonds, although I've never understood the difference. Or maybe it was floating a loan. You know how stupid I am about those things, so why keep asking me about it? Anyway, it doesn't make any difference now."

Was she lying to me? I could not tell. All I knew was that it would do no good to keep questioning her. She would continue to retreat into vagueness. I said, "It's just that you seem to have something on your mind."

"Well, life isn't very pleasant these days." She added swiftly, "Now don't start talking about going back to New York. I know the American ambassador could arrange it, but I don't want to go. Here we at least have a pleasant place to live. And as soon as the war is over, we'll have plenty of food."

"The war won't be over until the Prussians get what they are asking for—Alsace and Lorraine."

She waved her hand. "Two little provinces. Pooh! What are they? Surely not worth all this suffering. Soon the government will decide to be sensible."

No use to tell her that the government was more frightened of some of its own people than of the Prussians. At the first sign that the government might surrender, thousands of rioting Parisians, including armed National Guardsmen, would fill the city's streets. But my mother, safe so far in her fine house, would never believe that.

I looked up to see that Madame Duchamps had come noiselessly into the room. We sat in silence until she had taken away the plates. Then my mother said in a fretful tone, "I have never liked that woman. She moves as quietly as that cat of hers. She can come right up behind you without your knowing it."

She added, "I wish we had Victor and Annette back."

"So do I."

Victor and Annette Lavalle, cook and housekeeper respectively, had been with my mother for nearly all of the seven years she had lived in this house. Then last June a Right Bank restaurateur had offered Victor a post as chef at an excellent salary. The Lavalles, like my mother, had wept when they left, but they had left.

The next day Madame Duchamps had appeared. She had heard in a neighborhood shop that there was a position open. She would not ask for much in the way of wages, if her nieces also were given employment. Philippe had hired her on the spot.

Apparently my mother, too, had been remembering that. She said, with a wry smile, "Philippe always wanted to save money whenever he could."

Madame Duchamps came back with the coffee. There

72

was no dessert. There had not been for many weeks. When the housekeeper had left us, I said, "Will you go to bed early tonight? You look exhausted."

"No use to go to bed if I can't sleep. I'll stay down here and read until I begin to feel drowsy."

I myself went to bed soon after Madame Duchamps cleared the table. Almost immediately I fell asleep.

Sometime later I came groggily awake, aroused by a sound that might have been the front door opening and closing. Then I heard my mother's low voice in the entry hall. A caller? But what caller, especially at this time of night? Then I realized it need not be very late. I had gone to bed before nine. And probably the sound I had heard had not been the opening and closing of the door. Probably Madame Duchamps had come up to consult my mother about something or other and, while there, had turned the heavy key in the front door lock. I went back to sleep.

A scream from somewhere below penetrated those layers of unconsciousness. My mother's scream, abruptly broken off at its highest pitch. I sat up, heart drumming with terror, and swung my feet out of bed. Automatically snatching up my robe, but not putting it on, I ran out into the hall. At the head of the stairs the robe trailing from my hand tripped me, and I had to clutch the rail to keep from falling. Then I raced on down the curving stairs. Halfway down I became aware that the ground floor door stood open. When I reached the lower hall, I saw that half the courtyard gate was swinging closed.

In the salon doorway I halted for an instant. In the green gown she had worn at dinner, my mother lay crumpled on the floor about fifteen feet away, one cheek

73

pillowed on her outflung arm. Something gleamed in the light. The pearl handle of a letter opener, protruding from the back of that green gown.

I don't remember running across the room. I just remember kneeling beside her. The twitching of her eyelids told me that she was alive. "Mother!"

Someone else was in the room. I looked around and saw Madame Duchamps in a blue flannel robe, her face white between two braids of graying dark hair. "Get Dr. Leclerc," I said. Thank God he lived only two streets away. "Don't stop to dress. Get him!"

Not speaking, she hurried toward the hall. I turned back to my mother. "Who did this to you?"

Her eyes were open now, and looking up at my face, but an unfocused vagueness in their expression made me think she did not recognize me. She whispered, "Must see—Frederick Mosser first."

That friend of Philippe's who had seemed to admire her so much. "Was he here? Did he do this?"

Momentarily that unfocused look left her eyes. "Martha?" she whispered. "Martha?"

I said desperately, "Try to tell me. Who was here tonight?"

It was no use. That cloudy look was back in her eyes. "Fleur-de-lis," she said.

"Mother, please—"

"Take it to him." I saw that again her eyes had cleared. "Fleur-de-lis. You'll find it . . ." She broke off, as if aware that her words made no sense. Then, lifting her head slightly, she made one last effort to communicate. "Shield," she said. "Two-headed sheep." Then, more urgently: "Shield!" Her hand made a groping motion, as if to seize my wrist.

74

I cried, "Don't move!" Her head sank back on her arm, and her eyes closed. My gaze went to the handle of the letter opener, that pretty little knife which usually lay on that Louis the Fifteenth writing desk in the corner. Thank God that I knew, from my training at the ambulance, that it almost surely would be fatal to her for me to dislodge that knife.

I sat huddled there in my nightgown, my eyes going from her white face to the almost imperceptible rise and fall of her chest and then back to her face. I dared not rouse her lest she waste her strength in more senseless speech. And senseless it had been except for her reference to Frederick Mosser. True, this house was full of fleurs-de-lis. They were embroidered on draperies, carved on wall paneling here in the salon and the library across the hall, and painted on furniture. But there was no shield of any sort in the house, with or without the device of a two-headed sheep.

The minutes dragged by. Finally aware of the chill, I put on my robe, and then just sat there on the floor, my ears strained for the first sound of footsteps hurrying across the courtyard. As I looked down at my mother's white face, I kept seeing her as she had looked at times in the past. Happy and secure and oh-so-young one day when she and my father and I had gone to Delmonico's for luncheon. Pale with grief and financial worry in the weeks after the War Department telegram came. Excited and young once more the night of that backstage party, when I had helped her put on that pretty lavender evening gown.

Then I saw that it did not matter how long it took the doctor to get there. She had stopped breathing.

Chapter 8

Gray light, filtering through a dusty window, fell on the commissionaire's face. He could not have been much more than thirty-five, I realized, but in that bleak morning light he looked old—almost as old and tired as I felt.

He said, from the opposite side of his battered desk, "Then you are sure that you did not hear the ringing of the bell outside the courtyard gate? Only the opening of the front door, and then your mother's voice?"

"Yes."

"And she did not sound alarmed, as she would have been by the entrance of a complete stranger?"

"No."

"Perhaps she had expected the caller, and left the gate open."

It was an effort to speak. "Perhaps Madame Duchamps left it open."

He drew a sheet of paper toward him. "Ah, yes. Jeanne Duchamps, your mother's housekeeper. No doubt our men have questioned her and her two nieces. I see that they were questioned after you were attacked by an intruder last September second. They denied leaving the gate unbarred and the door unlocked, and denied all knowledge of the affair."

His words did not require an answer, and so I made none.

"And you are sure your mother made no statement about her assailant? She merely told you to 'take' something, something she did not identify, and then spoke some words that had no meaning for you, something about a fleur-de-lis and a shield?"

"She also mentioned Frederick Mosser."

"Ah, yes. And you assumed that she wanted you to take this something, whatever it was, to Monsieur Mosser, although she made no direct statement to that effect. Is that correct?"

I wanted to cry out, "I have answered these questions twice before." When Dr. Leclerc had arrived, he had knelt beside my mother for perhaps a minute, and then, rising, had led me gently to the far corner of the room. The police would be here soon, he told me. Before he left his house, he had sent a maid with a message for them.

A few minutes later, just as the first daylight was showing through gaps between the draperies, two policemen arrived. The younger policeman, a man of about twenty-five, questioned me in the library, and wrote down my numb answers in a notebook. Then he suggested, very politely, that I accompany him to the local commissionaire's office. Dr. Leclerc, who had come into the library to stand beside me, advised me to consent. "Best to go now." Dimly I realized that he meant it was best to go to the police station before this anesthetizing shock wore off. "And don't worry about—other matters. I will see to the funeral arrangements."

Now I answered, "That was all she said." I added,

with an effort, "And you will question Frederick Mosser?"

Although he did not move, he seemed to withdraw a little. "I have said so. You realize, of course, that Monsieur Mosser is an important and respected man. We cannot haul him down here like some ordinary suspect, especially when you yourself say that your mother made no accusation against him."

I thought of Frederick Mosser's talk of his citation from Louis Napoleon. He must be a clever man, I realized fleetingly, if he had influence in this new regime too. "But you have sent for Professor Richard, haven't you? I told you how he had kept hounding my mother, and how on the omnibus he—"

"You have told us, and he will be here soon. Now you say that you and your mother have lived in France for almost eight years."

"Yes."

"And that the house in which she lived is part of the estate of the late Baron Perruchot?"

I felt my jaw clench. "Yes."

The questioning went on for about five minutes. Then the office door opened and Professor Richard came into the room. I caught a glimpse of the sandy-haired policeman before he closed the door behind the old man. This morning he looked more unkempt than usual, and wild with fright. Like many frightened creatures, he launched an immediate attack.

"What is the meaning of this? Why have I been dragged from my bed at this hour? I, a member of the Academy of Sciences!"

"A thousand regrets, monsieur. Please sit down."

"I will not sit down!"

"As you prefer. But surely you were told that a lady of your acquaintance, a Madame Hathaway"—he glanced down at his notes—"a Madame Flora Hathaway, has been—"

"Yes! And I was shocked, deeply shocked, even though I had met her only once. But what has that to do with me? Why am I—"

"Mademoiselle Hathaway says you called at her mother's house repeatedly, even though her mother made it obvious that she did not want to see you. She says furthermore that on an omnibus recently you made a statement which she feels, in retrospect, might be construed as threatening."

"She lies! What statement?" The bright, wild gaze behind the spectacles swung upon me. "What statement?"

"You said to tell my mother that she must see you. You said your patience was wearing thin."

"I did not!" He turned back to the man behind the desk. "I said nothing about patience! And if I called upon Madame Hathaway several times, it was only because I hoped to find her in, so that I could offer condolences. I am of the old school, monsieur. No matter how irregular the connection, if it is of long standing, a true Frenchman offers sympathy."

He paused for breath, and then said, "Which of us will you believe, monsieur? This understandably overwrought child, or me, Jules Richard? Why, I have been an associate of Pasteur. Do you know the name of Louis Pasteur, monsieur?"

"Yes, I know it. You may go now, Professor."

With one last wild look at me, Professor Richard went out, closing the door behind him. I said, into the silence, "Then you are just going to let him go?"

"For the moment." He paused. "Old men can be obsessed by notions, such as that one of his about offering proper condolences. Besides, no doubt he is lonely. Lonely people welcome any excuse to make calls on others. As for his remark about losing patience—well, it is his word against yours, is it not?"

I understood then. Beneath my numb grief I felt the first stir of bitter rage. Professor Richard, however unkempt and eccentric, was not only French, but a man of some distinction. And I? I was the daughter of a foreign adventuress, a woman who had been kept for seven years by a man high in the inner circles of a deposed regime. Probably this Flora Hathaway, the man behind the desk must be thinking, had admitted a new lover to her house last night. There had been a quarrel . . .

Besides, Paris was ringed by enemies. At any hour they might storm the fortifications or launch a bombardment with their cannon. Should the police turn the city upside-down, and harass worthy citizens, on behalf of a woman who had not even been respectable, let alone French?

"You also may go, mademoiselle." As I stood up, he too rose. "Rest assured we will do all we can to apprehend this criminal."

I just looked at him.

He flushed slightly. Then, as if hoping to end the interview on a more amiable note, he smiled and said, "It would be best to tell no one what your mother said about the fleur-de-lis, and so on. Even though it is incomprehensible to us at the moment, it might not be to someone else. And there is no point in putting him on his guard, is there?"

80

"No. Good day, monsieur."

When I reached the house, Madame Duchamps admitted me. With dull relief I saw that she, or someone, had closed the door to the salon. She said, as I averted my gaze from that door, "Yes, they have taken her away. Oh, mademoiselle, what a terrible, terrible thing!" She paused. "You must be exhausted. Surely you will want to go to bed now."

"Not just yet. First I must talk to you."

Alarm leaped into her eyes. "About what, mademoiselle?"

"I intend to stay on here. But I want you to leave, right today. And take your nieces with you."

"But why?"

She already knew why. The alarm in her face had turned to consternation. I said, "Because it was your duty to see to it that no one can get into this house at night, or even through the courtyard gate. One night last September you left the gate unbarred and the door unlocked, and again last night."

"Mademoiselle, I swear! I know nothing about who did this terrible thing to Madame. And I did not leave the door unlocked, not . . ."

Abruptly she broke off. I said, "Not last night. Isn't that what you were about to say? Last September you left the gate so it would open, and the door too, but last night only the gate."

I pictured someone slipping into the courtyard, and then reaching through the window bars—with his stick, perhaps, or a twig from the mulberry tree—to tap on the glass. My mother must have looked out, seen a face she knew, and then gone to open the door—whether with reluctance in her heart, or a glad confidence, or mere curiosity, I might never know.

If her visitor last night had been the same person who invaded this house last September, why hadn't he, as on the first occasion, waited until we were all in bed? The answer was obvious. Last September he had failed to find what he sought. And so last night he had come here to question my mother about it. He could have been confident he would find her awake. Night after night the glow from those salon windows, a little taller than the courtyard wall, must have been visible from the street.

Madame Duchamps had recovered some of her poise. "You have no right to make such accusations against me, and no way of proving them."

No, no more than I could prove what Professor Richard had said to me on the omnibus.

"And as I told the police, I have no idea who assaulted you weeks ago, or who did this terrible thing to Madame last night."

That might be true. Whoever had bribed her might have remained anonymous. Perhaps on two occasions when she collected mail from the box inside the courtyard gate in the morning, she had found an envelope addressed to her, with money inside, and a hand-printed note promising more money if she would oblige the sender in a simple way . . .

"I know nothing!" she repeated. "Both nights I was in my room, sound asleep. Last night I did not come upstairs until your mother's scream awoke me."

Probably it was true that she had been in her basement room. Even if she had taken the bribe money, surely she would have wanted to shut herself in her room off the kitchen, keeping clear as much as possible of any consequences of her act.

Her voice was bolder now, as if she had become certain that I had no proof, only suspicion. "And if you dismiss us, how are we to live, eh?"

"The Baron's lawyer paid you a year in advance." I decided not to refer again to the bribe money. She would only have repeated her denials. Besides, my weariness was suddenly like a weight upon me, so heavy that I was no longer aware of my rage and my grief, but only of my need for rest.

"But what of my nieces? Your mother paid them little enough, God knows, but now they will not have even that."

"There is plenty of employment. The balloon factory, the uniform factories—"

"Such work takes nimble fingers. And Jeanette and Louise are both awkward girls, and easily flustered."

True. That was why only Madame Duchamps had served meals and cleared away the china and crystal afterwards.

"My nieces are fit for only the simpler kinds of kitchen work."

"Then let them do kitchen work!" I felt that I could not stand up for more than a few seconds longer. "There are plenty of jobs. Only the other day the woman who runs the café two doors from the ambulance said that she needed kitchen help."

Instantly I regretted my words. It would not be pleasant to see Jeanette's reproachful face, or Louise's, whenever I went into Madame Lamartine's. But then, I could not recall ever seeing any member of her kitchen staff in the outer rooms.

"Very well." Her voice was cold now. "We shall leave, immediately, and go to my sister in Menilmontant." She turned toward the rear of the hall.

Hand on the stair railing, I dragged myself up to bed.

Chapter 9

I awoke to find subdued sunset light filling my room. For a moment I felt bewildered. What was I doing in bed at this hour? Then realization, and grief, rushed over me like a flood of black water, so deep that I felt I might drown in it. But I must not. My mother's death had left me with a responsibility to carry out, no matter how long and discouraging the task.

Laboriously, as if I indeed moved against a strong current, I got out of bed and dressed. I decended to the shadowy ground floor hall. Madame Duchamps and her nieces must have gone. The house had an empty feeling.

In the basement kitchen I found unwashed dishes. The iron stove, upon which there almost always had been a *pot-au-feu* simmering, was stone-cold now. In Madame Duchamps' room and the one shared by her nieces beds were unmade and bureau drawers gaped, some with stockings and discarded undergarments dangling over the edge. No matter. At least she was gone, that woman with the cold, sly face I had never trusted.

I climbed to the ground floor. As I moved along the hall, I heard a subdued clamor. Someone had rung the bell outside the gate. As I crossed the courtyard to answer it, I saw that the clouds, stained with sunset colors, had begun to break up, revealing patches of pale wintry blue. Before opening the wicket, I lifted the lid of the iron box which, behind a slit in the gate, received mail. Yes, there was a letter in an unstamped envelope. I thrust the envelope into my skirt pocket and then opened the wicket.

John Lowndes stood outside, his brown head bare. Even now, in my leaden grief, I felt my throat tighten at sight of him.

I unbarred the gate. He stepped into the courtyard and waited until I had pushed the bar back into place. Then he said, "I have just learned what happened. It was in the evening newspapers."

To my relief, he did not say how sorry he was. I could not have borne sympathy just then, especially not from him. I said, "Come in the house."

In the library I lit a wall lamp and then, suddenly aware of how cold the room was, moved toward the fireplace. "Let me do that," he said, and dropped to one knee before the grate. While he assembled kindling, I opened the envelope and read the note inside. It was from Dr. Leclerc. He had arranged for a funeral the following Monday at a small Methodist chapel on the Right Bank. Internment would be at the Cemetery of Père Lachaise.

John Lowndes stood up. The first flames sent a rosy glow over the intricately carved paneled walls, over the shelves of calf-bound books which no one but me, probably, had opened for many years. Certainly my mother and Philippe had not. I sank onto a sofa and then said, "Please sit down."

He sat down in an armchair a few feet away. "I suppose you will return to the States now. If there is any way I can help—"

"I plan to stay here." At his surprised look I added, "Do you think I could leave, not knowing who . . ." I could not finish the sentence.

"But isn't finding that out a job for the police?"

I said bitterly, "Unless I am here to prod them, do you think they will try very hard in times like these?"

His silence told me that he did not.

"I am the only person left who loved her. And I'm the only one who really cares whether or not anyone every pays for . . ." Again I could not finish the sentence.

After a moment he said quietly, "I understand. But surely you don't intend to remain in this house."

"Yes, unless I am forced to leave." That well might happen, I realized. On his own initiative, or prodded by Baroness Perruchot and her son, Philippe's lawyer might say that with my mother's death I had lost the right to stay in this house another eight months.

"Will your mother's servants stay on?"

"They have already gone. I dismissed them."

"Dismissed them! Why?"

I told him, and then added, "I will feel safer here without them than with them. And I will feel as safe here as anywhere else. Wherever I lived in Paris, I would be alone."

And while I lived here, there would be no doubt that the gate was barred and the door locked each night.

"You plan to stay on at the ambulance?"

"Of course. I need the money." Besides, I scarcely could spend my days sitting in this silent house.

87

"Then you have no other money?"

His very bluntness robbed the question of offense. "My mother had some savings."

"In a bank?"

"No, here." Since that night last September, I had insisted that she keep her money, not in a bureau drawer, but in the salon safe. I also had made sure that she remembered to keep the safe locked.

"Is the money enough for your needs?"

"I don't know how much it is. I haven't counted it." I paused. "It's—across the hall, in the salon."

I saw understanding in his eyes. "Just the same," he said, "don't you think you should find out how much it is?"

"Yes, and I'd rather do it while you're—while I am not alone here."

I crossed to the salon and lit one of the wall lamps. How cold it was in there. Not looking toward the spot where my mother had lain, I took down the painting and opened the safe. Then, with the envelope of money in my hand, I turned out the light, closed the salon door, and returned to the library.

The envelope contained a little more than three thousand francs. No fortune, certainly, but sufficient to pay my mother's funeral expenses, with enough left over to buy such household necessities as coal and wood for the cookstove and the fireplaces.

He said, "But surely she left some jewelry. Perhaps if you need to—"

"You're thinking of the necklace and earrings she wore that night at the theater. Unfortunately, those are not mine to sell." Fleetingly, I recalled how I had

88

cringed at the sight of Baroness Perruchot's opera glasses leveled at that necklace.

He did not pursue the subject. Instead he said, "If you work all day at the ambulance, you won't be able to stand in the queues. How will you get food?"

"I hadn't thought yet, but I'll manage somehow. Perhaps the wife of the tobacconist in the next street will buy food for me when she buys her own."

"Then there is no way I can help you?"

"Not at the moment." I wanted to add that perhaps in the future he could, but pride forbade me. It would have sounded like a plea for him to keep in touch with me.

So that I could bar the gate behind him, I walked with him out the front door. As we crossed the courtyard, I said, "Did you receive my note thanking you for your gift?"

"Yes." He sounded suddenly constrained. "I would have called on you soon after I got back to Paris if I hadn't been so busy."

But not too busy to see Charlotte Vinoy, and probably more than once.

I said goodbye to him, barred the gate, and went back into the house. After I had locked the front door, I moved along the hall and descended the stairs to the kitchen. There in the thickening shadows I lit an oil lamp which stood on the wooden sinkboard. Neither Philippe nor any previous owner of this house had thought it necessary to install gaslight belowstairs.

As I had expected, Madame Duchamps had taken with her whatever small supply of food the vegetable bins and the larder had held. But far back on the top pantry shelf I found a package of tea and a tin with a few biscuits in it. That would suffice. I was not hungry. I would eat only out of the grim knowledge that otherwise I could not keep up the strength to do all that I had to do.

There was a little fuel left in the spirit lamp. Rather than waste precious wood and coal in the big stove, I used the lamp to heat water. I drank my sugarless tea and ate two biscuits. I made sure that the kitchen door, opening upon steps that led up to a narrow alleyway, was locked. Then I climbed toward the ground floor hall.

At the head of the kitchen stairs, I paused and looked at the door which had been cut into the rear wall of this house almost eight years ago. Although the door had been cut by Philippe's orders, I was sure that the idea had been my mother's. My poor mother, who had thought that by means of this door, and that "theatrical contract," she could pull the wool over the eyes of sophisticated Paris. The door stood locked and bolted, just as it had ever since that day last July when Philippe, accompanying Louis Napoleon, had taken the train out of Paris.

As I stood looking at the door, I was aware of the house's emptiness and of silence unbroken except by the ticking of the hall clock. I was aware, too, that the hour had come, that first hour when, with no other distraction, I would face my aloneness. The thought brought with it a certain relief. Now I could huddle before what remained of that fire in the library and wrap my arms around me and, if I needed to, rock back and forth in my grief.

On Monday afternoon, a comparatively mild afternoon of alternate sunlight and shadow, I stood beside the open grave in the Cemetery of Père Lachaise, head bowed as I listened to the prayer of the Methodist minister. It was strange to hear that prayer, so simple and Anglo-Saxon in its phraseology, spoken in the French tongue. Monsieur and Madame Bitizius, who had brought me to the church and to the cemetery in their carriage, stood beside the grave. So did John Lowndes, and two nurses from the ambulance who had Mondays off, and Dr. Leclerc. Madame Leclerc had not accompanied him.

As we had climbed to the gravesite, up flights of stone steps and along winding paths, I had realized that in life my mother probably had never visited Père Lachaise. She would have thought it a lovely spot. All around us, interspersed among the tall cedars, stood the monuments of France's illustrious dead, so that the steep hillside looked more like a vast garden of statuary than a place of mourning. Abelard and Héloïse were buried here, and Molière, and Balzac. So were many uncelebrated French, of course, and a few foreigners, both illustrious and obscure, who had died in Paris. And now Flora Hathaway, once the pretty and pampered small daughter of South Carolina gentlefolk, was to lie in this beautiful but alien spot.

A man detached himself from the group of gravediggers standing a few yards away and handed the minister a small shovel. The minister handed it to me. I scooped up a little of the raw earth and let it fall on the coffin. In the sound of that falling earth, as in the minister's words, there was something final, and yet comforting. In life driven hither and you, by ill luck and ill judgment, my mother was at rest now.

When we had gone through the wrought-iron gates at the foot of the hill, John Lowndes drew me aside. "Are you all right?"

Did he look at others with that closed, unreadable expression? I did not think so. "Yes, I am all right."

"Is someone buying food for you?"

"Yes, the tobacconist and his wife." Deprived of whatever small sums Philippe had paid them for the privilege of walking through their shop and back room, they had been glad to accept the three francs a week I offered.

"When will you return to work?"

"Tomorrow." And I would be glad to. Work would be a solace as well as a necessity.

He seemed to be hesitating. I asked, "What is it?"

"I don't know whether or not I should tell you, but perhaps I should. It's about Philippe Perruchot."

"Philippe!"

"Yes. While I was away from Paris, I heard a rumor that he is alive and in Berlin."

I said, bewildered, "You mean he was only injured? He's in a Prussian hospital?"

"No. According to the rumor, he was nowhere near that magazine explosion. The day before that he'd learned that the Emperor planned to question him about some sort of suspected disloyalty, and so he went over to the Prussians."

When I did not speak, he added, "Remember, it's only a rumor. I'm telling you only because I thought it might be of some importance to you, although I don't suppose it is."

No, it was not, really. Aside from his wife and son, probably the only person for whom that rumor would have had importance lay in that new grave up there. I said, "Thank you for telling me."

"Remember, if you have need of me, you can always get in touch with me through the *Observer*."

His meaning was clear. I would see him only if I had need of him. And by need he obviously meant something more concrete than this absurd and useless yearning in my heart.

He tipped his hat and walked away. Monsieur Bitzius handed his wife and the other two nurses and me into the carriage.

Chapter 10

On Tuesday morning, before reporting to the ambulance, I visited the commissionaire in his office with the dusty window. Yes, he said, the police had called upon Frederick Mosser. "But it is impossible, mademoiselle, that he could have been concerned in this tragic affair."

"Why? Because he is a man of such great respectability?"

He stiffened slightly. "Not only that. In early December he had the misfortune to slip on a patch of ice on the Rue Raynouard, near his house. Since then he has been confined to the indoors with a broken leg."

Rue Raynouard was in Passy, the western suburb where many of the city's richest men had bought old houses or built new ones during Louis Napoleon's glittering reign. "Are you sure he has a broken leg?" Anyone could stretch a bandaged, splinted leg upon a footstool. And inducing a wife or well-paid servant to give corroborative evidence might be no problem.

The commissionaire looked shocked, then angry, and then pitying. "Mademoiselle, I can understand how you might be a prey to morbid and suspicious fancies just now. But when our agents interviewed Monsieur Mosser, his doctor was present."

For a moment I was silent. "And you have learned nothing else?"

"No, but as I assured you, we are doing everything possible. And now, if you will excuse me . . ."

I wanted to say, as I stood up, "Very well, I will leave. But you are going to see me again and again until you do learn something."

In the early morning two days later I returned to him. Although I could sense his exasperation, he maintained his courtesy. No, there were no new developments. But I could rest assured . . .

On Friday morning, determined to find out for myself the state of Frederick Mosser's health, I crossed the river to the Place de la Concorde. For a sum equivalent to the cost of a day's food, I hired a closed carriage to take me to Passy.

After the comparatively mild weather the day of my mother's funeral, the bitter cold had returned. On the Champs-Elysées I saw that many of the trees, above their protective iron grills, had been stripped of bark. Near the Etoile I saw a gaunt, black-clad woman holding up a small boy so that he could break twigs from the tree's lower branches. An older boy stood at the curb, obviously ready to warn his mother and brother at the first sign of approaching police. Already the boulevards in northeastern Paris had lost their trees to people too poor to buy firewood. Now it was the turn of the better neighborhoods.

In Passy, though, there was little sign of suffering from either cold or hunger. Although smoke rose from the chimneys of the big houses set behind stone walls,

the trees lining the quiet streets had not lost their bark
to scavengers. The few carriages which passed held occupants snuggled deep into their furs. Even the coachman
appeared warmly dressed and well-fed. My own coachman asked a passing housemaid, her head wrapped in a
red woolen shawl, where Monsieur Mosser lived. A few
minutes later, leaving the carriage to wait in the street,
I walked through open grillwork gates and moved up a
yew-bordered path to the house. It was of honey-colored
stone, with three stories and a mansard roof.

The white-capped maid who answered the door asked
me to wait in the paneled reception hall. How deli-
ciously warm it was in there, after the bitter day outside.
From somewhere above I heard the gleeful laughter of
children, and then a woman's gently chiding voice.

The maid returned to say that Monsieur Mosser
would see me. She ushered me across a salon where
dwarf magnolia trees in white porcelain jardinieres per-
fumed the warm air and a fire burned in the grate
beneath the portrait of a smiling blond woman with a
small girl on her lap and a slightly older boy leaning
against her knee. Then the maid opened the door of a
book-lined room. I stepped past her, and the door closed
behind me.

Here, too, a fire burned. Frederick Mosser, in a brocade dressing gown, sat beside it, his bandaged right leg
stretched out on a footstool. The flames' light heightened
the color in his face, and made his thick blond mustache
and blond imperial look reddish.

"Ah, Mademoiselle Hathaway! It is good to see you,
even though I am sensible of what a sad time this must
be for you. Forgive me for not rising. I have suffered a
slight accident."

96

"I know. The police told me."

He winced a little at my Anglo-Saxon bluntness, and then smiled. "Please sit down." When I had taken a chair on the opposite side of the fire, he asked, "What can I offer you? Coffee? Perhaps mulled wine? In weather like this—"

"Nothing, thank you."

"Then let me tell you how shocked and grieved I was to hear the terrible news about your mother."

I murmured an acknowledgment and then said, "You know, of course, that my mother mentioned your name just before she—"

"I was told. Something about how she must see me, was it not? I am at a loss to explain it, mademoiselle, at an utter loss."

Was he lying? I could not tell. Naturally he had guessed the purpose of my visit as soon as my name was announced to him. He'd had time to rehearse that bewildered tone, that guileless gaze.

For a moment I sat in silence. The commissionaire had warned me not to discuss those confused last words of my mother's with anyone. But if I left the investigation of her death entirely to the police, I reflected bitterly, I might never know any more about it than I knew now.

"My mother also said something about a fleur-de-lis and a two-headed sheep."

"A two-headed sheep!"

I had watched him narrowly as I spoke. The puzzled astonishment in his face seemed genuine. But again, I could not be sure.

He asked, "What could she have meant?"

"I don't know. I hoped you might have some idea."

"I? I can think of no explanation, unless . . ."

"Yes, monsieur?"

"Perhaps all sorts of irrelevant memories pass through the mind of one dying. Perhaps she recalled visiting a display of oddities presented by that American showman. What is his name? Barnes?"

"Barnum—P. T. Barnum. And we call them freak shows. Perhaps you are right, monsieur." But remembering the confused, desperate urgency in my mother's eyes, I did not think that she was remembering some long-ago visit to Barnum's American Museum in the carefree long ago. "And you can think of no reason why she mentioned your name?"

"None. Unless . . ." He glanced at the closed door, and then went on in a lower tone, "I admired your mother very much. Even though I was an associate of the Baron's, if your mother had given any sign that she might consider me as a special friend and protector . . ." His crooked forefinger was stroking his mustache now in that masculine preening gesture. "Perhaps she was aware of that. Perhaps one could flatter one's self that in her last thoughts . . ."

His voice trailed off. I said nothing.

"Or perhaps she was thinking of you, left alone in the world." Still preening his mustache, he looked at me with a subtly altered expression. "Perhaps she thought that I might be of assistance to you, in a financial way or some other—"

"Thank you, but I am in no need of assistance." Although his taste might run to blondes, obviously he did not disdain brunettes. I stood up. "Thank you for seeing me, monsieur. Good day."

When the hired carriage left me in front of the Saint-Germain house, I hurried inside. On the way back from

Passy I had thought of a new weapon in my constant fight against the cold. For the past week I had spent nearly all my hours in the house before the library fire, venturing to the icy lower regions only long enough to cook food on the stove or spirit lamp, and to eat my sparse meals on the kitchen table. Because my bedroom fireplace did not draw well, on the previous Tuesday night I had hauled my mattress down to the library, placed it on some old draperies I had spread out on the floor, and made up my bed near the grate. Now it had occurred to me that blankets, hung across the top of the stairs, might block some of the frigid air currents that flowed through the house.

Standing on a stepladder I had brought up from the kitchen, I put up my blanket barricade. I winced as I hammered nails through the blankets' binding to the fine old wood above the stairs' archway. But in the French phrase, what would you, if you are determined not to freeze?

When I had finished with the blankets, I went into my icy bedroom and took my brown dress from the wardrobe, the same dress I had worn that night John Lowndes came to our box at the theater. Two days from now, on the afternoon of Christmas Eve, Monsieur Bitzius was giving a party at Madame Lamartine's café for the staff of his ambulance and one in the neighboring Menil-montant district. Friends and relatives of staff members had been invited too.

If my mother had died in ordinary times, I would have been revolted by the thought of attending a party so soon afterward. But these were far from ordinary times. And Monsieur Bitzius had promised roast chicken and even a rum torte. He had obtained the confection when he, as

99

a neutral, had been allowed to pass through Prussian lines on a trip to Geneva. My mother would have been the first to point out that to deny myself much-needed nourishment would be the most arrant folly. The party would continue from three o'clock until midnight, with the guests arriving and departing at three-hour intervals, so that not too many staff members would be absent from the ambulance at any one time.

The dress needed pressing. When I cooked my evening meal, I would also heat an iron on the stove. With the dress over my arm, I pushed aside the blanket barrier and went down the stairs. I had nearly reached the library when I heard the ringing of the bell outside the courtyard gate. My pulses quickened. Probably John Lowndes knew that Friday was my day off. Hurriedly I deposited my dress on a chair near my makeshift bed, closed the library door, and went out to the courtyard.

When I opened the wicket, I saw that Etienne Perruchot stood out there on the sidewalk, his handsome young face set, unsmiling. A closed carriage stood across the street. Through its window I saw his mother, sitting very erect and looking straight ahead.

I closed the wicket and unbarred the gate. When it swung back, he said, his face still stony under his curling dark hair, "Please forgive the intrusion. I must speak to you."

"Come in, please." As he followed me across the courtyard, I wondered apprehensively why he had come here. To demand I leave this house? Or merely to ask for the emerald earrings and emerald-and-diamond necklace?

I could not take him into the library, not with my improvised bed on the floor. For only the third or fourth time since my mother's death, I opened the salon door.

The big room, cut off as it was from even the feeble heat of the library fire, was bitterly cold. "Will you sit down, Monsieur Perruchot?"

"I prefer to stand, thank you." He paused. "Then you know who I am?"

"Yes." I thought it unnecessary to mention his close resemblance to his father.

"I am sorry indeed to have to bring up such a painful matter so soon after your bereavement." I felt he had rehearsed that sentence. "It concerns jewelry which originally belonged to my late father's mother, and which rightfully now is my mother's property—or rather, my property." He reached inside his coat and then held out a folded, official-looking document. "If you would oblige me by looking at this . . ."

I unfolded the paper and glanced through it. It was a document from Philippe's bank, stating that it had in trust the ownership of certain jewelry, "described herein below," and that it had now transferred ownership to Etienne Perruchot, Second Baron.

I handed the document back to him. "Certainly," I said. Before I turned toward the safe, I saw surprise in his face. What had he expected? That I would argue the matter?

I placed the picture on the floor and spun the safe's dial. When I had opened the door, I pushed the envelope of money aside. It was thinner, now that I had paid my mother's funeral expenses. I took out the flat leather case and handed it to Etienne Perruchot.

He snapped the case open, looked at its contents, and then closed it. "Thank you." He stood there with the case in one hand, looking oddly unsure of himself now. After a moment he said, "I extend you my sympathies, mademoiselle, in the loss of your mother."

I thanked him, and then hesitated. Perhaps that rumor about Philippe which John Lowndes had mentioned had not reached Paris. If it had, obviously it had been discounted, or even disproved, by Philippe's family and his associates. Otherwise the bank statement would not have referred to Etienne Perruchot as the Second Baron, nor would he have spoken of his "late father." Still, how was I to refer to the man he had known as his father and I had known as my mother's lover?

At last I said, "And you have my sympathy in your own recent loss."

He made a formal little bow. But still he did not wish me good day and leave. "It must be lonely for you in this large house."

My nerves tightened. Was he about to tell me that I could no longer stay here? If so, where could I go in overcrowded Paris?

He must have read my alarm, because he said quickly, "My mother and I will respect the provision in my father's will which gave you—or rather Madame Hathaway—a year's tenancy."

"Thank you very much."

Again he bowed, and then said, with a rush, "Forgive me, mademoiselle."

"For what?"

For believing that I would try to hold onto the jewelry, or even that I might have sold it?

He reddened slightly. "For—for the intrusion. Good day, mademoiselle."

Chapter 11

I saw Etienne Perruchot again less than forty-eight hours later. As I emerged from the operating room on the morning of December twenty-fourth carrying a bucket of used swabs in each hand, I almost collided with Philippe's son, standing there in the narrow corridor that separated the operating room from the ground floor ward. "Good day, mademoiselle. I have come to make a small contribution to the ambulance."

I looked at the envelope he held out. To judge from its thickness, its enclosed contribution could not be described accurately as small. "That is very kind of you. I think Monsieur Bitzius is in his office. Just go down the hall to—"

"May I not leave my contribution with you?"

"Of course. But as you can see, my hands are not free."

"Please allow me." He slid the pocket into the uniform I wore, an all-enveloping garment of dark blue cotton. Then he stepped back and said, "As I came through the ward, I heard two women talking of a party this afternoon."

"Yes, in a café down the street. We are all looking forward to it." In fact, so as not to waste any of my three-hour segment of the party by going to the Saint-Germain house to change, I had brought my brown dress to the ambulance and hung it in the small top-floor room where the nurses sometimes snatched a few minutes' rest.

"I hope you have a most enjoyable time." He bade me good day, bowed, and went through the open doorway into the ward. What a solemn young man! Didn't he ever smile? But he was handsome, really far more so than John Lowndes. And despite my being Flora Hathaway's daughter, he liked me. Otherwise, if overwhelmed by a need to contribute to this particular ambulance, he would have mailed his donation. I found that thought, as well as the warmth in his brown eyes, very pleasant indeed.

A little after two-thirty that afternoon I went up to the top floor room and changed to my brown dress. I felt an eager anticipation of the coming feast. The tea I had brewed that morning had tasted odd, perhaps because I had not washed the pot carefully enough the night before. Half a cup of it had left such a bitter taste that I had been unable to finish my breakfast toast. At noon I had found that Madame Lamartine, busy with party preparations, had closed her café, and so I'd been unable to have my usual bread and soup. Consequently, I was more ravenous than at any time during these past hungry months.

When with a group of other nurses I entered the café shortly after three that afternoon, I saw that the partition at the rear had been taken down. The room looked huge now, and quite festive, with artificial flowers on each of the many white-clothed tables, and paper streamers stretching from the gas chandelier to the smoke-blackened walls. In a small place left clear for dancing, a man sat at a piano, with an accordionist perched on a wooden stool beside him. As I moved between the tables searching for my place card, the musicians struck up a tune from the operetta I had attended with my mother and Marcel Ranier that early September night. Could that have been less than four months ago? That foolish but entertaining performance, and the well-dressed, well-fed audience which applauded it, seemed part of another lifetime.

To my surprise, I found that I was to sit at Monsieur Bitzius's left, at the largest table in the room. But then, he had found a number of ways, since my mother's death, to express tacit sympathy for me. He was already seated there, with our chief of nurses on his right. Her name was Violetta—Violetta Bernard—and probably no one who ever bore that name looked less violet-like. She was almost six feet tall, with wiry dark hair that kept escaping its pins, and a perceptible down on her upper lip. But she was an excellent nurse, cheerful with the patients, and scrupulously fair in her treatment of the other nurses. The two doctors from our own ambulance were at the table, and three other men, whom I knew must be doctors from the Menilmontant ambulance.

And Charlotte Vinoy was at the table. Every other woman in the room, no matter how poor, had managed to make or borrow some sort of party dress, or at least to add a festive note—paste earrings or a bit of ribbon— to her attire. Charlotte wore the sort of plain dark jacket and skirt she always wore. And yet, with her flashing eyes, beautiful complexion, and proud carriage she was easily the most striking woman there.

As I slid into my chair, I noticed, with a leap of my

pulses, that there was a vacant place beside Charlotte. Had she suggested to Monsieur Bitzius that it would be a nice gesture to invite John Lowndes? His *Observer* articles about Paris ambulances had brought many contributions from America.

"Ah, my dear Martha!" Monsieur Bitzius had turned to me, round face beaming. He introduced me to the doctors from the Menilmontant ambulance, and then said, "What we were just talking about will interest you. I have been telling Dr. Marcea here about certain old houses in the Faubourg Saint-Germain."

I smiled and took a sip of the mulled wine a waiter had placed beside my soup plate. Just as his English counterpart, the philanthropist Richard Wallace, collected French paintings, Monsieur Bitzius collected the histories of ancient Paris houses.

"The house in which you live, for instance. Do you know that a certain Duke de Crecy stayed in hiding there for two years during the Fronde? Mazarin's soldiers searched the house repeatedly, but never found him."

The Fronde, that confusing war back in the seventeenth century between the king and his Italian adviser on the one hand, and certain rebellious nobles on the other. I took another sip of wine. No matter what purists might think of mulled wine as an accompaniment to food, I found it warming and delicious. "Well," I said, "it is a large house."

"Not that large. My theory is that he had some secret means of leaving the house whenever soldiers arrived. During the Middle Ages and the Renaissance, many buildings were constructed with ingeniously hidden exits. Why, it was through such a concealed passageway that some members of the government escaped from the

106

Hôtel de Ville during last October's disorders."

He threw a hasty glance at Charlotte, as if recalling that as a result of those "disorders" several of her radical associates were behind bars. But he need not have worried. Charlotte, smiling up at John Lowndes, had not been listening. He greeted Monsieur Bitzius, acknowledged introductions to Violetta and the doctors, nodded smilingly to me, and then sat down beside Charlotte. Well, I resolved grimly, the sight of him beside Charlotte was not going to spoil the feast for me. Nothing could do that.

The room was full of noise and movement now. Talk and laughter made a continuous din. The musicians had struck up a polka, and couples threaded their way through the tables to the dance floor. Monsieur Bitzius kept leaping to his feet as guests came up to greet their host.

"Good day, mademoiselle."

I looked up. Jeanette, the elder of Madame Duchamps' round-faced nieces, stood beside me, a steaming tureen of soup cradled in one arm, and a ladle in the other hand. So she had come to work here at Madame Lamartine's cafe. Her face and voice betrayed no resentment over my dismissal of her from the Saint-Germain house. In fact, she was smiling. Probably, I reflected, she was pleased to be away from those gloomy basement rooms and her aunt's sharp tongue. As she ladled soup into my plate, spilling some of it onto the cloth, I asked, "How is your aunt, and your sister?"

"Louise is working here too. And my aunt has a fine place with a rich family over in Passy. At first they didn't want her to keep Seraphine, but finally they said yes."

She stood there, smiling, with the soup tureen tipped

107

at a dangerous angle. I said in a low voice, "Hadn't you better serve the others before the soup gets cold? And watch the tureen. It's about to spill."

She nodded, still smiling, and moved on to serve the slim, olive-complexioned man at my left. He was Dr. Henri Rolland, a native of France's Prussian-bordered province of Lorraine, and a recent addition to the ambulance's staff. The soup was onion, that humble fare long favored by French working people and shunned by the prosperous. It was delicious. I wondered if the French middle classes had any idea of what they were missing.

Dr. Rolland gave an appreciative sigh. "Such wonderful soup."

"Marvelous." It had been made with a rich beef stock and, if I was not mistaken, real cream. As I took another spoonful, I noticed that John and Charlotte's chairs were vacant. I turned toward the dance floor. They were waltzing, the tall American and the beautiful, almost as tall French girl. Would he ask me to dance? Probably, if only out of politeness. I would refuse, of course. Attending this rare feast so soon after I had lost my mother was one thing. Dancing would be quite another. I turned back to my soup and finished it, wishing there was more. But just as well there was not. Chicken was to follow, accompanied, the rumor was, by green beans in a mushroom sauce.

A waiter had appeared to record our preferences for dark or light meat. I chose light, but nearly everyone else at the table asked for dark. Dr. Rolland said, "Monsieur Bitzius, I hope those chickens you ordered each have four legs."

Again seated beside Charlotte, John Lowndes said,

"Why not? If P. T. Barnum could find a two-headed lamb, surely the ingenious French should be able to find four-legged chickens."

A two-headed lamb. How strange that he should say that. And who else had mentioned the American showman? Oh, yes, his name had come up during my conversation with Frederick Mosser only two days before. I could not remember our exact words. In fact, I was beginning to feel very strange, my thoughts somewhat blurred, and a distinct queasiness in my stomach. Had I taken too much of the mulled wine? Or was it that soup, so much richer than anything I had eaten for many weeks? But I would *not* be ill, not with chicken yet to come, let alone rum torte.

Monsieur Bitzius said, "Ah, young Perruchot, is it not? Welcome, welcome!" With my queasiness subsiding momentarily, I watched the middle-aged man and the young one shake hands. "Waiter, please bring a chair for the Baron."

"Thank you. I have just finished a large meal with friends at a restaurant, but—"

"But you will have some wine with us? Good, good. And thank you for your generous contribution this morning."

"It was nothing."

Monsieur Bitzius laughed. "I would scarcely call it that. How very much you look like your father. I would have known you anywhere. Your father and I were acquainted, you know. In fact, it was through him that I met Mademoiselle Hathaway's mother."

He broke off, his round and rosy face looking appalled, as if he had just remembered that the father of the young man he addressed had been my mother's protector. For the second time in half an hour he had, as the English say, dropped a brick. But indeed he had met my mother when Philippe had invited him to the Saint-Germain house the previous June. I, newly returned from the convent school, and loathing the fact that I must live beneath the roof Philippe provided, had sat there in almost total silence. Then Monsieur Bitzius had begun to talk of his ambulance. I had asked eager questions, sure that joining his staff would provide me with a sense of usefulness and a measure of independence.

The waiter had brought a chair. "Where would you like to sit?" Monsieur Bitzius asked.

"Right here, if you don't mind," Etienne Perruchot said.

When he had sat down between our host and me, he said, "You look charming, mademoiselle."

It was pleasant to be told so, and pleasant to see that warm look in the brown eyes fastened upon my face. Nevertheless, I did not feel in the least charming. Another wave of queasiness had struck me.

"Would you care to dance before the next course is served?"

"No, thank you."

"I understand. Forgive me for asking. One could scarcely expect you to dance so soon after—"

"It is not just that. In fact, monsieur"—his face and everything in the room seemed to swim before my eyes —"in fact, I fear I am going to be most dreadfully ill."

Dr. Rolland was looking at me. He leaned toward the chief nurse. "Get her back to the ambulance, quick."

As hands assisted me to rise, I looked across the table. John Lowndes was on his feet, looking at me. But he did not come around the table. It was Violetta Bernard and Etienne Perruchot who guided my wavering footsteps between the tables. Outside in the darkening street the scarecrow figure of Professor Richard seemed to swim before my eyes. Had he been waiting out here, or had he followed me from the café?

"Mademoiselle Hathaway! I must talk to you."

Etienne's arm tightened around my waist. He said angrily, "Can't you see, you imbecile, that Mademoiselle is ill?"

The scarecrow figure seemed to vanish. Etienne and Violetta took me into the ambulance. At the foot of the stairs she must have told him not to come any farther, because as nearly as I can remember, it was she alone who half-dragged me up two flights to the little room where I had changed into my party dress. I recall falling onto the narrow bed, and then, moments later, being copiously sick into a basin.

I slept after that, woke to be sick again, slept, and again awoke and was sick. It must have been sometime toward morning when I became aware that Dr. Rolland's thin face was looking down at me. "How often has she vomited?"

I heard the voice of one of the night nurses. "Three or four times."

"She ought to be all right." His voice was moving away. "I told Bitzius it was risky to give half-starved people all that rich food."

I slept again, only to be awakened by the sound of the door opening. I lifted my eyelids and saw pale winter sunlight filling the room. One of the day nurses stood with her back to the door she had just closed. *"Joyeux*

Noël," she said sardonically.

Yes, it must be Christmas morning. I mustered a feeble smile.

"How do you feel?"

"Weak." And all my muscles ached.

"No wonder. They say you threw up everything but your *matrice.*"

Again I managed to smile. I had become used to the sometimes ribald humor of my fellow nurses. "Monsieur Bitzius," she went on, "says to tell you he is sorry, and that he realized you probably won't want to have Christmas dinner with him and Madame Bitzius."

He was correct in that assumption. I felt that never again would I want to eat. The nurse said, "But he will send a hamper to your house this afternoon." She paused. "We'll be needing this room, you know. Do you think you can go home now? There's a hired carriage waiting outside."

Thank heaven. I could not have faced the thought of riding in an omnibus with all the windows closed. "Did Monsieur Bitzius—"

"I don't know who hired it. Come on. I'll help you dress."

Dressing was a simple matter, since Violetta had managed to strip me only of my party gown before I toppled onto the bed. I put on the dark green jacket and skirt I had worn to the ambulance the day before. With the paper-wrapped brown silk dress under my arm, and still feeling weak and lightheaded, I went cautiously down the stairs and along the ground floor ward. The men lying or sitting up in the narrow beds greeted me with unwonted cheerfulness. It was Christmas, and they had special food to look forward to.

The coachman outside climbed down from the box and opened the door for me. I asked, "Would you please tell me who hired you?"

He shrugged. "I don't know his name. But he was a young fellow about twenty-one or so, dark-haired, good-looking. He told me to wait until you came out."

It had been foolish of me to hope that John Lowndes had ordered the carriage.

Chapter 12

The ride across the river, with the sound of church-
bells sweet on the cold, clear air, revived me somewhat.
But I was still so weak when I reached the house that I
did not kindle a fire immediately. Still wearing my cloak,
I sank onto a chair near the library grate.

My gaze wandered from the cold ashes in the fireplace
to my makeshift bed. I stiffened, no longer aware of the
dull ache throughout my body or the sweat of weakness
on my upper lip.

So as to keep up some standard of civilized housekeep-
ing—despite the extreme cold, despite my solitude—I
had made my bed carefully each morning, tucking the
sheets between the foot of the mattress and the wide
drapery I had spread out on the floor. Now the wrinkled
ends of the sheets hung free.

Still seated, I gazed around the room. A book I had left
lying on a table near the fireplace was no longer there.
I could imagine a searcher taking down all those vol-
umes, stacking them on tables and on the floor, and then
returning each of them, including the one I had been
reading, to the shelves.

Filled with growing anger and alarm, I got up then

and began to move from room to room. With all night in which to work, the intruder obviously had tried to leave no evidence of his search. But almost everywhere there were little signs. The salon safe was locked, and when I opened it, I found that the money was still there, but the envelope lay, not where I remembered leaving it, on one side of the safe near the door, but so far back I had to reach for it. Several pictures hung slightly askew. A small one, I saw, was loose in its frame. I took it down and turned it over. The backing had been pried loose at one side, as if the searcher had seen some evidence—perhaps a bulge in the thin wood—that something had been concealed between the backing and the canvas. Aware now of how meticulous the search had been, I scrutinized the furniture. No upholstery had been removed or even loosened, but in numerous places—on sofa backs, chair seats, and footstools—there were broken threads, as if someone had probed with a small, needle-sharp instrument.

In my mother's room the telltale signs were more numerous, perhaps because the searcher had spent more time there, or perhaps because he felt, quite rightly, that this room was so full of poignant memories for me that I visited it as seldom as possible. The bed's lace coverlet hung closer to the floor on one side than the other. Her hatboxes, which she always kept on the lower shelf of her wardrobe, now stood on the upper. In the top bureau drawer her linen handkerchiefs lay, not in their pink satin folder, but in a neat stack beside it. The white fur rug beside her bed lay askew. And when I bent to straighten it, I noticed that the deep hem of a blue satin window hanging had been unraveled at one end.

When I went down to the basement, I could not tell

whether the rooms once occupied by Madame Duchamps and her nieces had been searched. Unwilling to spend more time than absolutely necessary in that icy lower region, I had made no attempt to straighten the wild disarray those three had left behind them. But in the kitchen I saw that the oil lamp stood, not on the wooden sinkboard where I was almost sure I had left it, but on the table. And in searching the canisters the intruder had spilled a few leaves of precious tea on the floor.

It was fragments of glass, mingled with the tea leaves, that made me turn and look at the window. So that was how he or she had gotten into the house. In the window's upper half, a small pane of glass had been shattered. Obviously he had reached through the jagged opening, turned the latch, and then raised the window's bottom half. After leaving the house, he had lowered the sash, reached through the broken pane, and turned the latch. Plainly he had hoped that, finding the window locked, I would not guess that someone had invaded the house. Instead I would think that some rock-throwing small boy had shattered that pane.

Leaving the kitchen, I climbed three flights of stairs to the attic, a region I had visited only once or twice in all the years my mother had lived in this house. Light filtered through a large dusty skylight onto a wilderness of crates and barrels and carpet rolls and broken furniture. I did not need to venture farther than the doorway to see that the searcher had been here. To erase his footprints, he had cut irregular swaths in the floor's thick gray dust, probably by dragging after him the piece of ragged tapestry lying just inside the doorway. Those footprints, I realized, might have given an indication of the intruder's sex and height, and whether or not he had some peculiarity of gait.

I went back to the library and sat motionless beside the grate. Not just too much mulled wine then, or a too-rich soup. Something had been dropped into my wine, or into my soup plate—something non-lethal, but poisonous enough to insure that I spend the night at the ambulance. I was certain of that, although there was no way in the world of proving it.

Who had done it? Monsieur Bitzius, who sat on my right, and Dr. Rolland on my left, would have had the best opportunity. But others at the table, on their way to and from the dance floor, had moved past me. Guests from other tables, coming up to greet their host, had stood close beside me. And there had been the waiter, of course. With or without his connivance, something might have been added to the wine even before he set it beside my plate.

For that matter, Jeanette could have dropped something into my soup plate. But it was hard for me to imagine that such a clumsy, good-natured girl would have the deftness, let alone the ill-will, to do such a thing to me.

What should I do? Leave this house which, even in this terrible winter, provided me with comforts and a privacy I could not find elsewhere, even if I had the money to buy them? Perhaps I should appeal to Monsieur Bitzius. But although I felt he might be willing to take me into his home, Madame Bitzius would not. She had three daughters, the eldest of whom was eighteen. And although she had been kind to my mother and me, even inviting us to dinner, she had not followed the usual custom of summoning her daughters downstairs to pay their respects to her guests. It was unlikely indeed that she would want Flora Hathaway's daughter living beneath the same roof, day after day, as her own girls. And anyway, I would never risk embarrassing her and Monsieur Bitzius, and myself, by making such an appeal to them.

And then I suddenly realized that I was far safer now than I had been at any time since that attack upon me in the darkened salon last September. Last night the intruder had provided himself with enough time to search the house from top to bottom. Perhaps he had found what he sought. If not, he had been forced to conclude that it was not here. In either case, he would have no reason to return.

But tomorrow I would go to the police, I resolved grimly, and insist that they go over this house as thoroughly as the searcher had. Perhaps then they would find some means of identifying the person who, the second time he had invaded this house, had left my mother lying crumpled on the floor.

Putting my cloak aside, I knelt before the fireplace and began to arrange paper and kindling in the grate. As the first flames licked upward, I heard the door knocker strike. It was not until then that I realized that after the hired carriage had left me, weak and lightheaded, in the courtyard, I had failed to bar the gate.

I went to the door. At least I had remembered to turn the key in the lock. I grasped the key and turned it halfway. Then, even though I had just convinced myself that last night's intruder would not return, I hesitated.

"Mademoiselle Hathaway?" It was Etienne Perruchot's voice.

I opened the door. He said swiftly, "Forgive me. If you were lying down, I will go away."

"No, I feel much better now." That was true. Evidently my anger had had a tonic effect, because sometime during my survey of all the rooms in this house, my nausea had disappeared, and the ache in my muscles had subsided to a faint discomfort. "Come in, please."

He followed me into the salon. "Please don't remove your coat," I said. "It is very cold in here." I paused. "And thank you for ordering that carriage. It was very kind of you."

"Not at all."

We sat in silence for a few moments, I on a sofa, he in an armchair. Then he burst out, "Have you no servant?"

"No."

"Aren't you afraid, all alone in this house?"

"Less now than before." When he looked at me inquiringly, I said, "Someone searched this house last night," and then described the evidence I had found.

He said, looking both puzzled and appalled, "And nothing was taken?"

"I don't know. Perhaps." My voice hardened. "Perhaps he found what he came to get the night he killed my mother."

"Mademoiselle!" He appeared stunned. "Are you sure it was the same person?"

"Doesn't that seem logical? Certainly it was no ordinary thief who came here last night. An ordinary thief would have taken at least the dining room silver and the money I had left in the safe. And no ordinary thief would have searched so thoroughly, and then tried so hard to cover up evidences of his search."

He looked down at the floor, frowning. "Mademoiselle, you must not stay here."

"Where do you suggest I live? In some sixth-floor room with a broken roof, and rats? Although," I went on, smiling, "the rat population has been depleted of late, hasn't it?"

Oddly enough, it was the wealthy, not the poor, who had added rat to their menus. Although many Belleville National Guardsmen, when not manning the fortifications, had amused themselves and added centimes to their pockets by hunting rats, it was only the well-to-do who could afford the rich sauces needed to make such food palatable.

He did not return my smile. "At least you must hire a servant."

"With what?"

"I would be honored to loan you a sufficient sum."

Evidently a young woman alone in Paris could attract would-be benefactors of more than one age group. First there had been Frederick Mosser, and now this man only a year or so older than myself.

"You mean give, don't you? How could I repay such a loan?"

He reddened slightly. "Very well. Give."

"But surely you realize it would be impossible for me to accept such an offer."

His color deepened. He said stiffly, "Mademoiselle, I did not mean—"

"I am sure you did not," I said, although I was not sure at all. But I found myself warming to him, this serious young man whose formal manners were contradicted by his ardent brown eyes. If I had not met John Lowndes

120

first, perhaps I would have found Etienne Perruchot very attractive indeed.

We sat for perhaps thirty seconds in silence. Then he got to his feet. "I will leave you now, mademoiselle. I am glad that you are no longer ill."

"Thank you, monsieur. You have been very kind."

It was not until he had gone that I realized he had not commented upon one thing—the intruder's apparent knowledge that I would be absent from the house all night. Well, perhaps the thought had not occurred to him.

Early in the afternoon Monsieur Bitzius's coachman arrived. He brought my Christmas dinner in a napkin-covered hamper, and a note suggesting that I give myself a chance for full recovery by staying home the next day. While the coachman waited, I wrote a reply. I thanked him and said briefly that the house had been broken into the night before, but no great damage had been done. The details could wait until I returned to the ambulance.

That morning I had thought that I would never desire food again. By five in the afternoon I was so ravenous that it was with difficulty that I restrained myself from eating all, rather than more than half, of the small roast chicken, crusty bread, and slice of rum torte in the hamper Monsieur Bitzius had sent.

Chapter 13

The next morning I went to the commissionaire's office. Exasperation flitted across his face when he saw me, but his greeting was polite enough.

As I told him of my sudden illness Christmas Eve, and of the broken basement window I had found the next day, and the little signs left throughout the house by a determined searcher, I saw a weary, ironical look growing in his eyes. When I had finished my account, he said nothing until I prompted, "Well, monsieur?"

"Mademoiselle, I am sorry that the food at your party disagreed with you."

I said, too taken aback even for anger, "Is that all you think it was?"

"But of course. Rich food, the kind most of us have become unaccustomed to, eaten too rapidly."

"And someone just happened to choose that particular night to search my house for—"

"Mademoiselle, you yourself say nothing was taken. As for those 'signs' of yours, are you absolutely sure you made your bed in a certain way that morning? Can you recall the exact moment when you folded the sheets under the mattress?"

"Of course not. One doesn't remember the exact moment one does something habitual."

"Nor the exact moment when, perhaps because of some preoccupation, such as an anticipated party, one neglects a part of one's routine. And can you swear that you had left your money in a certain part of the safe, or that the picture had not been loose in its frame for some time?"

I was beginning to feel the first doubts. "But the disarrangement in my mother's room—"

"Are you sure that she herself did not rearrange her hatboxes? It has been my experience that ladies are always rearranging things."

He had the aggrieved tone of a man married to an habitual furniture rearranger. Perhaps recently, coming home in the dark, he had fallen over a footstool his wife had moved to a new location that day.

I said, "But the broken window in the kitchen."

"Someone searching for food. In these days people are driven to steal food, even people who would not dream of taking anything else. And on Christmas Eve, a man with no treat for his family the next day might very well be tempted to break into the kitchen of a rich-looking house."

"I had no food, except an ounce or so of tea, and some bread. And that was not taken."

"Many French people never drink tea. And very few would bother to steal bread."

That was true. Two commodities remained both plentiful and cheap—bread and wine.

I said, after a moment's silence, "And the way the dust was disturbed in the attic? Do you have an explanation of that?"

"I do. You have told me that you dismissed your mother's servants. They would have had trunks or boxes stored in the attic. The poor, mademoiselle, take all their possessions with them wherever they go. And women would have dragged anything heavy across the floor, rather than lifting it. That was less than ten days ago, not long enough for the dust to resettle."

Would I, that day after my mother's death, have heard them dragging their possessions across the attic floor and down the stairs? Probably not. Exhausted by the terrible night just past, and by my interview with the police and that unpleasant session with Madame Duchamps, I had slept like one drugged until sunset.

Evidently the commissionaire had seen my discomfiture, and had decided to press the advantage. "Mademoiselle, I am sensible of what makes you so determined that the one responsible for your mother's death will not go unpunished. But in turn I hope that you are sensible that these are difficult times for everyone, including the police, and may become more so. Or are you aware that observers on our fortifications have seen Prussian cannon moving closer to Paris?"

"Of course I am." Accounts of the new threat had appeared in newspapers, often accompanied by editorial reassurances that the enemy was bluffing.

"Even so," I said, "I trust that you will be able to send someone to inspect the house."

"But of course, mademoiselle. This very day."

After I left him, I collected my day's food supply—two carrots, an ounce of lamb, and a long loaf of bread—from the tobacconist's wife, and then crossed the street to the glazier's shop. He assured me that in the morning he would replace that broken pane of glass. Then I went home, and with growing self-doubt again inspected the salon furniture. Had those minute snags been there all along?

Seraphine! I had forgotten all about her and her needle-like claws.

Early in the afternoon two policemen arrived. One was the sandy-haired young man, the other an older man I had never seen before. Embarrassed now, convinced that I had made a fool of myself, I first showed them the broken basement window, and then led them over the entire house. The younger man wrote busily in a black notebook, but they asked few questions and made no conjectures.

I was at the door, bidding them goodbye, when a young boy leading a brown-and-white dog of indeterminate breed walked through the open gate. "Mademoiselle Hathaway?"

"Yes." Puzzled, I moved across the courtyard to meet him. He reached inside his jacket, brought out an envelope, and handed it to me. As soon as I had unfolded the note inside, my eyes went to the signature: John Lowndes.

He had written, "I stopped in at the ambulance late yesterday. Bitzius told me that you were better and had gone home, but that you'd found evidence of a prowler. Here is some prowler insurance. His name is Samson, and his former owner is a *London Times* correspondent who is going home next week. Samson has learned to subsist on anything, I am assured, including stale bread.

"Best to keep him indoors when you are not at home, so that he can repel intruders, and so that there will be less chance that he will end up on someone's menu."

Feeling dazed, I took the leash the boy handed me, and

looked down at Samson. He grinned back at me, and waved a plumy tail. He was more collie than anything else, I decided. The two policemen also were inspecting my new acquisition. The younger one, with the air of a man who likes dogs, bent to pat the shaggy back. The older man eyed Samson's fairly plump sides with the expression of a man who had learned to like dogs in quite another sense.

I thanked the boy, again said goodbye to the police, and led Samson into the house. When I had closed the door behind me, I reread John Lowndes's note. It was nice that he had taken the trouble to inquire about me at the ambulance. It was nice that he gave me such unusual but practical gifts—first a wedge of cheese, and now a watchdog. But since he never made his gifts in person, I found it hard to be properly grateful.

Chapter 14

When the first Prussian shells crashed onto the Left Bank about ten days later, I did not know about it. None of us at the ambulance knew until an excited woman of the neighborhood rushed in to tell us. Several shells had plowed up earth in Montparnasse Cemetery, where, as one of the nurses remarked with grisly humor, "they couldn't have bothered anybody." But six women standing in a food queue had been killed, and one little girl on her way home from school.

The next day more iron missiles hurtled down, all on the Left Bank. According to observers on the ramparts, the Prussian guns could not reach the other side of the Seine. And so I was not surprised on my way home that evening to see people, obviously residents of cheap and poorly constructed Left Bank houses, streaming across the bridges carrying their possessions with them. I considered only momentarily the idea of joining them. The house where I lived, like all of the old mansions of that neighborhood, was of massive stone construction. As the newspapers had pointed out that morning, such structures could survive any amount of shells with no greater damage than shattered windows and a few chunks of stone knocked from their walls.

That night I lay on my makeshift bed, sleepily aware of Samson's warm bulk at my feet. The first night after he joined my Spartan household, I had placed an old blanket in the hall, and tried to make it clear that he, like any proper dog, would sleep on his own bed. He had scratched and whined at the door until I, needing my sleep, had admitted him to the library. After that, of course, it had been the old story of the camel with his head in the tent. For two nights he slept on his blanket, spread between my bed and the fireplace. The next night he moved closer to the mattress. The night after that, and from then on, he slept across the foot of my bed. Chagrined as I was by my failure as a disciplinarian, I found it a delightful novelty to go to sleep with warm feet.

I had just dozed off when a tremendous crash somewhere nearby brought me bolt upright. Samson, barking wildly, dashed to the closed door, ready to deal with whatever danger threatened. Another crash, farther away this time, and then another and another. Was this to be the pattern from now on—night bombardment? If so, there would be a lot of tired people going to work each morning.

For three or four hours the crashing noises continued, accompanied by Samson's thunderous barks. Then silence settled down. I managed to sleep a little before the dawn light awoke me.

About an hour and a half later, as I turned off Rue Ramponeau and climbed the side street toward the ambulance, I saw Charlotte Vinoy moving toward me with her graceful stride. She stopped and asked, "Did the bombardment keep you awake last night?"

128

"I managed to get a little sleep."

I think she scarcely heard my answer. With a strange blend of anger and exultation in her dark eyes, she said, "It is good that the bombardment has begun. Now people will demand another sortie out of Paris to silence those guns. And this time the National Guard will take part."

It was on the tip of my tongue to say "God forbid!" There had been a second sortie some weeks before. Like the first, it had ended with wounded and dying brought back into Paris on omnibuses and river steamers. I felt that even the most humiliating surrender would be preferable to another such attempt. But then, it was not the capital of my country which was besieged. If it had been, perhaps I would have felt the same fiery determination to resist.

I asked, "What does John Lowndes think about another sortie?"

"John? I don't know. I haven't seen him since that party at Madame Lamartine's."

For a moment I was silent. "Then you and he . . ." I broke off, feeling warm color in my face.

Her smile, amused but not unkind, told me that already she had guessed how I felt about him. "Yes, that is over. Such things don't last, you know. One does not take them seriously."

Perhaps she had not taken it seriously. But had he? So seriously that he could not feel any real interest in any other young woman? I said, "Well, goodbye. I am already late." I walked on toward the ambulance.

More than eight hours later I left the first of the two omnibuses which carried me from Belleville to Faubourg Saint-Germain each night. A little group of people stood there on the corner in the path of light from a shop window. The nearby street light was dark. Because coal gas was needed to inflate the balloons which still sailed out over the Prussians' heads, street lamps often remained unlit.

As I stood there, I felt a hand on my arm. I turned and saw Professor Richard. Even in that dim light I could tell that his beard was as unkempt as usual, and his clothing as rumpled. "Mademoiselle!" His low voice, too, was as agitated as it had been the last three times we met. "I must speak with you."

I moved with him several yards away from the group of people. "First of all, mademoiselle, I apologize for accosting you on the street that afternoon you were ill. I had come to the ambulance expressly to see you, and I was so worried that at first I did not perceive—"

"After the way you lied at the police station, I am surprised that you should approach me anywhere."

"Forgive me, mademoiselle. I dare not be questioned by the authorities. I dare not!"

I looked at him wearily, wanting only to get home, cook and eat my scant meal, and fall into bed. "What is it, monsieur?"

"Have you had time to go through your mother's papers?"

I had, two days after her death, although "papers" seemed a pretentious word for the pitifully few letters and documents she had accumulated. Because she had no Paris friends to correspond with, or to receive invitations from, the desk in the salon had held only unused letter paper, advertisements torn from newspapers, and dressmakers' and milliners' bills, all marked "paid." In a small rosewood box on the bureau in her room I had found her marriage license, letters my father had written during his few months as a Union soldier, the War Department telegram announcing his death, and letters I had written to her while at the convent school.

"Yes. I have gone through her papers."

He glanced over his shoulder and then said, in an even lower voice, "Did you find a paper with numbers and symbols on it?"

"A *what?*"

"Please, mademoiselle. Please keep your voice down. It was the record of an experiment I made at the Baron's laboratory over a year ago. It was a failure, a shocking failure."

"What does this have to do with—"

"The Baron told me to abandon that sort of research, and to say nothing to anyone about it. I was only too glad to promise that. He kept my record of the experiment. That was his right, of course, as my employer. I thought nothing about it at the time. But later, after I heard the news of his death, I realized that such a record, if it fell into the wrong hands—"

"I don't know what you're talking about. What experiment? What record? And why should it be among my mother's papers?"

"I thought the Baron might have left it with her for safekeeping. He would not want to leave it in his home, or his bank, or his business offices. And as for the nature of the experiment," he said, his tone suddenly lofty, "that is a scientific matter, and beyond your comprehension."

After a moment I asked, "Did you search my house for that paper?"

"I? Never!" He recoiled as if struck, and then reached

out to clutch my arm. "Did someone search your house?"

"I am not sure. The police think not."

Even in that uncertain light I could see that his face had whitened. "Perhaps it is already too . . ." He broke off and then said, "If you tell the police about this conversation, I shall deny it ever took place. Do you understand, mademoiselle?"

I certainly would tell the police. But I doubted that they would do anything about it. With shells dropping on Paris, and with daily riots in the food lines, and street brawls between groups of bored and drunken National Guardsmen, the police had enough to do without questioning an old man they must consider at least a little mad.

"I can safely deny it," he said. "The Baron is dead. I worked without an assistant at the laboratory. I always worked alone there."

That I could understand. It was hard to imagine any capable assistant putting up with the cantankerous Professor for more than a few days. I was silent for a moment, and then said, "You mentioned something about 'the wrong hands.' Did you have anyone especially in mind?"

"No! No one!"

"Do you know a man named Frederick Mosser?"

"I do not! Why do you mention him? Has this man approached you since your mother's death?"

"No. I went to see him."

"Why? Did your mother give you some message for him?"

I looked into his distraught face. If I told him that indeed my mother had given me the impression that she had something for Frederick Mosser in her possession, something that she wanted me to find and turn over to him, the old man might collapse at my feet from sheer fright. At the very least, he would be strengthened in his delusion that my frivolous mother had been involved in something that constituted a danger to himself.

Was it a delusion? Remembering her blithe assurance of last September that soon she would have a large sum of money, and remembering her confused dying words, I certainly could not ignore the possibility that she had been involved in some intrigue dangerous, not only to herself, but to others, perhaps including Professor Richard. But investigating that possibility was a task for the police, not this semi-hysterical old man.

I said, "She mentioned his name when she was dying. I thought there might be some reason she wanted me to see him. But when I went to his house, he said he could think of none."

I looked at the approaching omnibus. From its windows, in other times ablaze with light, came the feeble glow of one or perhaps two oil lamps. The four horses which drew it were no longer sleek and plump. But then, as I often reflected when I saw those gaunt horses dragging their burden through the streets, they were lucky to have escaped the city's ovens and stewpots. "Good night," I said, and hurried toward the corner.

The omnibus had carried me only a few hundred yards when, looking wearily out the window, I suddenly stiffened. A tall, well-dressed man had turned the corner onto a side street, affording me a glimpse of a handsome profile under the brim of his hat. Philippe Perruchot? It couldn't be! As the omnibus carried me across the intersection, I turned around on the seat and looked back, but already he was lost to my view among other pedestrians.

I settled back in the seat, convinced that I had been mistaken. Even assuming that rumor about him was true, it could not have been he turning that corner. If indeed he had gone over to the Prussians, he had betrayed not only Louis Napoleon, but France. I could not imagine any concern urgent enough to make him risk returning here to a cold, hungry, bombarded city which was far more bitter against the Prussians than it had been when he left it.

That night I was in bed before eight o'clock. When the distant crash of the first shell awoke me, I ordered Samson to stop barking. I think I must have slept several minutes before the next crash, followed by Samson's low growl, again awoke me. After a while the shelling stopped, and I was able to sleep without interruption.

Chapter 15

Shells continued to plummet down all that next week, most of them at night, but some in the daytime. Carrying no explosive charge, the iron missiles did no great damage to either property or life. Deaths from disease and war wounds still far outstripped the toll from the haphazard shelling. Once Parisians saw that the rain of missiles did little damage, some of them began to regard the bombardment as a kind of entertainment, a distraction from the hunger and the cold. Each night a crowd gathered in the Place de la Concorde to watch the shells plunge down across the river.

On Friday afternoon of that week I returned to the Left Bank after a long and useless wait in a food queue. There had been a rumor that a butcher near the Place Vendôme would be selling a large supply of rabbits, by the ounce. Real rabbit, not cat. Since it was my day off, I had decided to try my luck. Whether or not the rumor was true I never found out, because the butcher closed his shop while there were still at least twenty women ahead of me in the line. At another shop I bought two soup bones, one with quite a lot of beef left on it, and then started home.

When the omnibus let me off on Boulevard Saint-Germain, I turned onto my narrow street and then stopped short. A small crowd had gathered in front of the closed gate of my house. Such groups always gathered before a shell-damaged building. But surely no shell had pierced the solid exterior of that particular house.

I hurried forward, and made my way through the crowd. A National Guardsman in the uniform of one of the Left Bank companies stood before the latched gate. "I live here," I said. He unlatched the gate and let me through.

Someone had tied Samson to the trunk of the mulberry tree. At sight of me he began to whine and to strain at the rope, forefeet pawing the air. I patted him, told him to be quiet, and then crossed over the cobblestones to another Guardsman stationed at the door. I asked, still incredulous, "A shell?"

He nodded. "Right through the skylight, like threading a needle. The Prusskies couldn't do that again even if they tried."

The skylight. When I judged this house invulnerable, I had not taken into account that glass area in the roof. We went inside and stood in the salon doorway. The missile had plunged through the attic and through the bedroom beneath it, leaving a jagged hole in the salon's lofty ceiling. Shell fragments, as well as glass from two shattered windows, lay on the Savonnerie rugs and the brocaded furniture. Like some bit of sculpture on display, one curved shell fragment stood on its edge atop the rosewood writing desk.

I asked, "When did this happen?"

"Around eleven this morning. Are you the owner?"

"No, a Monsieur Perruchot owns this house. Baron Perruchot, I should say. Has he been notified?"

"I suppose so. The owner always is." He paused. "Are you going to go on living here? The owner can have that skylight and those windows fixed in no time at all. And you wouldn't have to use this room, or the one the shell came through upstairs."

"I shall certainly stay here, if the owner permits."

"I don't blame you." His admiring gaze traveled over the carved wall paneling and the fragment-littered furniture. "I'd stay here even if the roof was never fixed. Well, I'll leave you now. The man will stay on the gate for a while, until the crowd leaves. Some of those youngsters might try to climb over. Which reminds me, better get your dog inside."

"I intend to."

After I had bade the Guardsman goodbye, I freed the deliriously grateful Samson and led him inside. With the dog padding after me, I went down to the kitchen and placed the soup bones in the larder. Then we went upstairs. The shell had plunged through the center of a bedroom two doors from my mother's, a room we had never used. I had just returned to the first floor when the knocker sounded. Etienne Perruchot, almost certainly. I shut Samson up in the library and then opened the front door.

He said, his young face as serious as ever, "Good day, mademoiselle, although I fear it has not been a good day for you."

"Nor for you, since it is your house." I opened the door wide. "But come and see. It is not too bad."

In the salon he looked at the hole in the ceiling, and

137

at the shattered windows. "I am told that the shell came through the skylight. I shall have it repaired tomorrow, and the windows too."

"Thank you."

"Of course, repairing the other damage will take longer. I realize you would not want to stay here, with the house in this condition, and workmen all over the place."

I opened my mouth to speak.

"Now I know what you are going to say," he hurried on. "But this time you must let me supply you with money for temporary lodgings. As owner of this house, I am responsible."

I smiled. "For what the Prussians did? And I wasn't going to say I had no money. I was going to say that I don't mind in the least staying here, if the skylight and windows are to be repaired immediately. As for the other repairs, I won't even see the workmen, since I am away all day."

He looked at me silently for a moment, a baffled expression in his dark eyes. Then he bent and removed a shell fragment from one chair, and several fragments from another. "Mademoiselle, may we sit down? I must talk to you."

I sat down on one of the chairs. He sat on the other one for several silent seconds, and then rose and began to pace up and down, apparently not caring that he ground glass fragments into the rug. "If it had not been for this accident, I would not have come here today. But I would have come here sooner or later. Ever since our last meeting . . ."

He stopped and faced me. Suddenly I realized, feeling

stunned, that perhaps he was about to propose marriage. And if so, what would I do? Accept him, or, like a fool, go on wanting a man who didn't want me?

"Mademoiselle, I know that what I have to say will come as a surprise to you, because you are of course aware that I knew what your mother was. My mother and I realized it more keenly than anyone in Paris! But it is also obvious that you have escaped her moral taint."

As I looked at him, speechless with astonishment and outrage, he went on, "I know that my mother would be horrified at the thought of any connection, even an— informal one, between us. Her attitude will constitute a problem. We can hope that in time, though, she will see you as I do. Besides, I am of age, and free to follow my own wishes." Again he paused. "Well, mademoiselle?"

I said, from a constricted throat, "Well, what?"

"Have I not made myself clear? I am asking you to do me the honor of becoming my wife."

Several seconds passed before I could speak. "I think you have made it obvious which one of us you think would be honored. But unfortunately, I must refuse."

His face went blank with astonishment. "Refuse!"

"Exactly."

The blood rushed to his face. "May I ask why?"

I got to my feet. "In the first place, I could scarcely accept a man who had just insulted my mother. In the second place, I don't love you."

He looked at me, astonishment still mixed with the growing anger in his face. Then he bowed very low, turned, and crossed the room.

In the salon doorway he turned back, his face now pale. "So that the weather won't do more damage to this house, I shall have the skylight and windows repaired tomorrow. But for the other repairs I shall wait until the end of your tenancy."

In my indignation I had forgotten that the roof over my head, whatever its condition, was his property. "I shall search immediately for another place to live."

"Oh, please don't, mademoiselle." From the relish with which he spoke, I knew that he had expected me to say that, and had prepared his riposte. "These days untenanted buildings are broken into. By staying, you will save my mother and me the expense of hiring a caretaker."

He went into the hall. I heard the outer door open and close.

For a moment I stood there, trembling with anger. Then I went into the library and sat down. While Samson rested his head on my knee and rolled worried eyes upward, I tried to decide what to do. Did self-respect demand that I leave surroundings that were more comfortable than I could find elsewhere? And not only more comfortable, but safer, now that I had Samson?

The knocker sounded. Was he back again? With the dog moving beside me, I went out into the hall and opened the door.

"I am from the *Observer*, madame. Would you care to tell our American readers in your own words what it is like to have a Prussian shell land in your parlor?"

I laughed, hoping that my face had not betrayed my gladness at seeing him there. "Come in," I said.

In the hall he stopped to scratch Samson behind the ears. "He looks fine. What do you feed him?"

"Bread, soaked in broth, or stew, or whatever I've prepared for myself. And he gets soup bones after I've cooked them, although I'm afraid that by that time they do little more for him than exercise his teeth." I paused. "Did you really come here to write about this particular shell?"

"No, but when word came in that Baron Perruchot's house was hit, I thought I had better come to see if you were all in one piece."

"I am, but the shell isn't."

We moved into the salon. He looked at the jagged hole in the ceiling and whistled softly. "Sit down," I said. When we were seated on the chairs Etienne Perruchot had cleared of shell fragments, I asked, "Would you like some tea? I'm afraid I have nothing else."

I had not expected him to accept, and he did not. "No, thank you. I never drink tea."

After a moment I said, "I met Charlotte Vinoy on the street the other day. She said she had not seen you for quite a while."

If Charlotte's name evoked any strong emotion in him, his face did not betray it. "Yes, I've been quite busy. Speaking of meeting people, I quite literally ran into young Perruchot on Boulevard St. Germain, or rather, he bumped into me. He looked pretty distracted. I doubt if he even recognized me. He must have been thinking about that shell."

"No, not the shell." I found my heart beating fast with the anticipation of telling him.

"What, then?"

"He had just asked me to marry him."

I saw astonishment in his eyes, and, fleetingly, some other emotion. I could not identify it, except that I had a gratified sense that it was not unmixed pleasure. Then he smiled and asked, "Will I be invited to the wedding?"

"There will be no wedding. I refused him."

"Refused!" Etienne himself had sounded only a little more dumbfounded by that word. "Good God, girl! Have you lost your mind?"

My sense of elation died. I said coldly, "His proposal was insulting. Perhaps he didn't mean it to be, but it was. He—he said things about my mother, and pointed out that his mother would be horrified by any connection between himself and me, and then added that nevertheless—"

"All right, he was tactless. But it is hard for even a Frenchman to be tactful and honest at the same time, and he was being honest. You couldn't expect him not to resent your mother, could you? And you certainly don't think he'd expect his mother to burst into cries of joy at the news you were to be her daughter-in-law."

He paused. When I remained silent, he went on, "But think, Martha. You're alone in the world. Here's a man with money and even a title who wants to marry you. And the young pup is good-looking enough, God knows. Most girls would be happy to settle for even half that."

"I don't want to have to settle for anything!" I said, half incoherently. "I—I want to have control of my own life. I want to be able to choose!"

I longed to add, "Give me a chance to choose *you.*" But I was afraid to, and not just because women were not supposed to say such things. I was afraid of seeing an appalled look in his eyes, and of hearing him stammer out that although he liked me, he had never thought of me in terms of marriage.

He said, "You're a strange one. Even men often can't choose. They have to settle for what they can get in life.

And women almost always have to settle."

My mother had said something like that before we had gone to the theater that night last September.

He went on, "Are you going to continue to live here, now that you've turned down your landlord's marriage proposal?"

"I don't know." I was aware that my tone was what my mother would have called sullen. "I haven't decided yet."

"I'm not sure, but there may be a vacant flat soon in the house where I live, on the Rue de Odette. A widow who lives there with her young son may move to her parents-in-law's house. You would be much nearer your work."

So that was where he lived. It would indeed be nearer my work. Although the Rue de Odette was middle-class, it was on the edge of Belleville, and within walking distance of the ambulance. Too, if we saw each other every day, perhaps in time . . .

"What you should really do," he said, "is go back to America. I could still help you arrange it."

"After I've hung on this long?" Had he become tired, I wondered bitterly, of feeling more or less responsible for me, an almost penniless compatriot of his?

He sighed. "No, I didn't suppose you would go home." After a moment he added, "Have the police learned anything more about your mother's death?"

"No." I had gone to the commissionaire's office that morning before crossing the river to join the food queue. His politeness was wearing thin. He listened with barely concealed boredom while I repeated Professor Richard's remarks about a "paper" he thought might have been in my mother's possession. Finally the commissionaire said that he would "look into the matter." I was sure he would not.

The thought of that last conversation with Professor Richard reminded me of the man I had seen on the street a few minutes later. I said, "Have you heard anything more about that rumor concerning Philippe Perruchot?"

"No. Why do you ask?"

"Two reasons. First, I thought I saw him on the street a few nights ago."

He smiled. "That isn't very likely, even if he's alive."

"I realize that. The second reason was that you mentioned Etienne Perruchot having a title. If his father is still alive—"

"Officially he's dead, and as long as he is, his son is the Baron." His smile turned wry. "Too bad you refused him. That haughty look you have sometimes would go very nicely with the title of baroness. Well, I had better get back to my desk."

I saw him out the door. Then I went down to the kitchen and, watched by ravenous-eyed Samson, put the soup bones on to boil.

Chapter 16

Two weeks later I found in the mailbox a letter from John Lowndes saying that the widow and her son had decided to keep their flat. But by that time Paris was in such desperate straits that I felt almost ashamed of my sharp disappointment.

The city was facing utter starvation now. Even bread had been rationed, and it was of such miserable quality —black, heavy stuff made of mildewed flour, beans, rice, and heaven knows what else—that Samson would drop it on the floor, look at me pleadingly, and pick it up only when he was convinced I had nothing more palatable.

As hunger increased, so did the demands of street corner crowds that the government launch another attempt, this time with the National Guard taking part, to break through the iron ring of besiegers. Late in January the government complied. The sortie ended in another shattering defeat, with the ill-trained, ill-equipped National Guard taking the worst losses. As the other nurses and I worked far into the night caring for the wounded that omnibus after omnibus brought to the ambulance door, I had little doubt that France would have to surrender.

Two days later the armistice terms were announced.

France would have to elect a new government, with which the victors would settle the final peace terms. In the meantime, the Prussians would allow food to come into the starving city.

Food from England, free for those with no money to pay for it, soon began to arrive. Other food flowed in from the provinces for sale in the shops. Although not cheap, it was less expensive than before. I bought a leg of lamb, from which Samson and I feasted royally for almost a week.

But in areas like Belleville, the free food soon ran out, and prices were still so high that housewives could buy only the coarsest food offered by the shops. Many of the children, I knew, still went to bed hungry. And in Madame Lemartine's café, I more than once heard Charlotte Vinoy, these days usually with a bearded young anarchist poet beside her, prophesy bitterly that the lot of the French workers would grow worse. In the new government, she said, they would lose even the small influence they had in the present one.

She was right. The new Deputies, elected not just by Paris but all of France, were overwhelmingly middle-class in their sympathies. As their head they chose an old man named August Thiers, whom the workers had long regarded as their worst enemy. The peace terms he signed with Bismarck included one particularly humiliating provision. The victorious Prussians would march into Paris, spend the night there, and march out again.

I saw that triumphal entry. Along with thousands of silent Parisians, I stood in mockingly bright March sunshine and watched the victors stream down the Champs Elysées. I could not help finding it a magnificent spectacle. Stirred by the music of the many bands, cavalry horses danced over the pavement and arched satiny necks. Sunlight glittered on steel helmets, gold braid, and on the spears a company of uhlans carried in their saddle sockets. They looked so proud, those well-fed, splendidly uniformed young men, that each one might have been a conquering prince. But I was careful to keep appreciation of their appearance out of my face, and later I learned it was fortunate that I had. That day mobs tore the clothing off several women who had expressed too openly their admiration of the victors.

Soon after the Prussians marched out, thousands of Parisians had new cause for despair. In poor neighborhoods and even those of the lower middle class I saw groups of bewildered-looking people standing on sidewalks beside their furniture. According to Thiers' new law, returning landlords, who had fled Paris before the siege to spend the winter comfortably in the provinces, could evict tenants unless all of the back rent accumulated over the past terrible winter was paid immediately.

And so I was not surprised—only dismayed and sickened—when the storm broke.

I was in the ambulance that mid-March day when the sound of gunfire came from the direction of Montmartre, that high ground on the northeastern edge of the city. Almost instantly the ambulance was full of rumors. The Prussians had returned to renew the war. No, it was merely target practice. No, Thiers had sent the one regular army unit left in Paris to wipe out the National Guard.

In the midafternoon, while I was changing the leg bandage of a man wounded in that last disastrous sortie, I looked up to see John Lowndes standing beside me.

"Finish that." His face was white. "Then meet me outside."

A few minutes later I faced him in the small vestibule. "What has happened?"

"All hell has broken loose."

He told me that Thiers indeed had sent the soldiers available to him up to Montmartre. Their mission was to recover cannon which the National Guardsmen, afraid that the Prussians would seize them during their triumphal march through Paris, had dragged up onto the heights. The Guardsmen, acquiescent at first, had been persuaded to resist by several radical leaders, including Charlotte Vinoy, who had joined the growing crowd. And not only the Guardsmen had listened. One after another the soldiers Thiers had sent reversed their rifles and shouted, "Down with Thiers! Long live the National Guard."

"Things got out of hand after that," John said. "The old general who'd been in command of the soldiers was declared a prisoner, and hustled down to the National Guard post in the Rue de Rosiers, trailed by a mob that was mostly women. You know the sort of female vultures who gather when there's a promise of bloodshed in the air."

I did know. The lowest sort of prostitutes, aged alcoholics, and vengeful crones thirsty for any kind of violence. I could imagine them surging down the semi-rural street, past the houses with their gardens filled with flowers and early vegetables.

"They began howling for the execution of the old general. The Guardsmen and Charlotte and the others tried to argue with the mob, but it was no use. The old man was dragged into the garden, beaten up by the crowd, and finally shot. The women—well you don't need to know what happened to the old man's body."

Sickened, I leaned against the wall. "What does it all mean?"

"It means that the Thiers government is through. There are not enough loyal soldiers left in Paris to sustain it. They say that Thiers and his ministers have already fled to Versailles."

"And—and now?"

"Paris will be run by a commune. I imagine that radical leaders have already gathered at the Hotel de Ville."

Commune. It had a dreadful sound, conjuring up history-book memories of that revolution nearly a century before, with tumbrels rumbling through the streets, and old women knitting in the Place de la Concorde as the guillotine blade made its whirring descent.

"The point is, you should not try to go home tonight. There'll be disorders all over the city. Is there a place here where you can stay?"

"Yes. But Samson is shut up in the house. He'll have no dinner—"

"Go get the key. I'll see that he's fed."

When I handed him the key a minute or so later, he said, "I'll leave it on the north side of the base of that tree in the courtyard, under the vines."

I watched him hurry down the street, that tall, strange man who kept appearing in my life and then disappearing. I wondered how much time would pass before I saw him again.

Chapter 17

Strange as it sounds, the biggest change in my personal life during the first week or so of the Commune was that I resumed sleeping in my bedroom. A blackbird —not the raspy-voiced creature we Americans call by that name, but a sweet-singing European blackbird— began a nest in the courtyard mulberry tree, and that convinced me that winter actually was over. I tugged my mattress up the stairs, pausing to rest every few steps, and restored it to my bed. Otherwise my life went on as before. I went to the ambulance, came home, fed Samson and myself, and then either read or sat out in the courtyard in the lingering twilight.

I continued to visit the commissionaire's office. There was a new commissionaire now. He was a little less polite than the old one, but equally uninterested in the death of a woman who had been not only a foreigner, but the mistress of a man high in the councils of a detested former regime.

Etienne Perruchot did not appear, nor did any workmen arrive to mend that hole in the salon ceiling. That did not matter, since replacement of the skylight and the salon windows had made the house weatherproof. I had long since given up the quixotic notion that honor demanded my vacating these premises. As Etienne had pointed out so scathingly, I was saving him and his mother a caretaker's wages. If they continued to see the matter in that light, and apparently they did, then so would I.

During my leisure time I wandered about Paris. There was a holiday spirit in the soft spring air. In the Place de la Concorde and on the Rue de Rivoli I sometimes saw Belleville residents I recognized walking along with bemused delight in their faces, as if seeing for the first time the full splendor of their city. In the Luxembourg Gardens children of all classes played beneath the newly leafed trees, and at night a band supplied by the Commune played patriotic and light classical music.

The ominously titled Commune was behaving with astonishing mildness. No one's property had been confiscated. Money belonging to the Thiers government had been left untouched in a bank, even though Thiers himself had announced that he intended to destroy the "rebels" in the Hôtel de Ville. The most radical thing those Communard leaders had done so far was to rescind that cruel law demanding immediate payment of all back rent.

They seemed to be a gabby lot, those Communard leaders. While militants like Charlotte Vinoy kept urging them to send the National Guard to Versailles to arrest Thiers and his deputies, those men in the Hôtel de Ville went on making long, philosophical speeches at each other, all of which appeared in the newspapers.

Early in April those first dream-like days of the Commune came to a shattering end. Once more shells rained down on the city. Thanks to those windy philosophers in the Hôtel de Ville, Thiers had been allowed time to rally army units from other parts of France.

Ironically, it was in the most staunchly pro-Thiers neighborhoods, the fashionable Passy and Auteuil districts, that most of the Versailles army's missiles fell, but others reached the heart of Paris, knocking chunks out of the Arc de Triomphe. In face after face I read the bitter thought, "Now it is other Frenchmen who are trying to destroy Paris."

But what really seemed to poison the air that lovely spring was the knowledge that many well-to-do Parisians felt a secret joy at the thought of Thiers' troops taking over the city. Distrust was everywhere, like a miasma. On the omnibuses I noticed that most of the usually voluble Parisians rode in silence, now and then darting quick glances at fellow passengers from the corners of their eyes.

One Thursday I came home to find a letter in the mailbox. Recognizing the handwriting on the envelope, I tore it open with eager fingers. He had something to tell me, John Lowndes had written. Would I meet him for lunch on Friday at the Café Leban?

I dressed carefully the next morning in my best day-time clothing, a jacket and skirt of blue bombazine. There was no need to take the omnibus. The café was just across the river. Besides, it was a beautiful sunny day, with a light breeze stirring the leaves of the mulberry tree.

When I started across the bridge, though, I found it was not a breeze sweeping down the river, but a brisk wind. It whipped at my skirts, and loosened a strand of my carefully arranged hair. John must not see me like that. At the far end of the bridge, within a hundred yards of the café, I stopped, took from my reticule a little silver-framed mirror, and propped it against the base of a lamp standard on the balustrade. Bending slightly, I looked into the mirror and began to tuck the errant strand into place.

I heard someone cry, "Look! She's signaling."

Startled, I turned around. Two women and a man, fear and rage in their faces, were moving toward me from the other side of the bridge. I sensed rather than saw that another group of people, coming onto the bridge from the Right Bank, had quickened their pace. The man with the two women said, "Filthy spy!"

I stood there, utterly bewildered. Within seconds, it seemed to me, a sizable crowd had collected. I heard someone ask, "What is it?" and someone else give the incredible answer, "They've caught a spy. She was signaling to the gunners."

The idea was ludicrous. The Versailles gunners were miles to the west, beyond the Bois de Boulogne. They could not have seen the flash of a tiny mirror.

I found my voice. "This is absurd. I was only—"

"Listen to that accent! She's a Prussian!"

"She worked for Bismarck, and now she's working for Thiers."

A young boy darted forward, seized the mirror, and held it high. "Evidence!" he shouted. "Evidence!"

There were at least fifty people around me now, some merely staring, others shouting and shaking their fists. I stood there with the stone balustrade pressing against my back, and fear growing in my heart. These people had been tormented for months by hunger, cold, loss of loved ones, and iron missiles raining down, first from Prussian guns, now from guns manned by other French-

153

men. No wonder they were half mad with hatred and suspicion.

The boy who had seized the mirror had raced away. Numb with terror now, I thought of the street crowd which weeks earlier had lynched a man some passer-by had accused of spying. They had thrown him into the Seine and beaten him with barge poles until he drowned.

I said desperately, "I am not a Prussian. I am not a spy. I was just . . ."

I broke off. A head taller than any of the others, he was shoving his way through the crowd. He put his arm around me, and then shouted, "Listen, my friends. She is not a Prussian. She is an American, just as I am. Do you hear me? American!"

Except for a few mutters, the uproar subsided. They eyed us uncertainly. America was well thought of in Paris. It had been the first country to recognize the Republic after Louis Napoleon's fall.

"What's more," John Lowndes said, "she has worked all through the war at an ambulance in Belleville. Don't you believe me? We'll all go up there, and you can talk to the doctors and nurses. Don't be afraid. She won't get away. There are a lot of you, and she's only one girl."

Now many faces held embarrassment. Several people turned to walk away, then several more. The woman who had first shouted at me said in a defensive tone, "But what was she doing here on the bridge with that mirror?"

"I suppose what a woman usually does with a mirror. I hope she was trying to make herself pretty for me." He smiled at her. "She and I were to meet for luncheon."

She looked at me, a kind of resentful apology in her eyes. Then she and her companions moved on.

154

The crowd had melted away entirely now. John said, taking my arm, "Don't hurry. Stroll. If that youngster who dashed off comes back with some of Rigault's men, we don't want to appear suspicious."

He meant Raoul Rigault, a priest-hater and avowed Terrorist who, because of the poisonous distrust pervading the city, had risen to power. As head of an organization which ferreted out "suspected traitors," he had thrown thousands into jail, including an aged archbishop and a number of lesser clerics.

We moved slowly off the bridge and along the quay. But when we had turned onto a side street, he hurried me forward a few yards. We made our way swiftly through sidewalk tables to the interior of the café.

When we had sat down at a table, he ordered two Pernods. Then he just sat and waited until my labored breathing became normal. When I began to tuck strands of my disordered hair into place, he said, "I had hoped to tell you I had found a flat for you not far from the ambulance. But this morning I learned it will not be available. Nevertheless, you must move. Already it's too dangerous for you to be crossing Paris every day."

My voice still sounded shaky. "I've been all right until today."

"You won't be all right during a street war."

"Street war!"

"Exactly. Why do you think they have started to build street barricades in the western part of the city? Even those dreamers in the Hôtel de Ville are realizing that Thiers will never negotiate with them. He's going to force his way into Paris."

The waiter approached. We sat in silence until he had placed two glasses before us and turned away. Then

John said, "There are two bedrooms in my flat. You had better move into one of them."

Too startled to answer, I merely looked at him.

"We can have it annulled when all this is over, but we'll have to be married, for form's sake." He added, smiling, "Besides, my concierge is a real stickler for the proprieties."

I said dazedly, "Married?"

"Probably we'll seldom see each other. That extra bedroom has a separate entrance from the hall. And the kitchen will be all yours. I never use it."

I said, still not sure that this conversation really was taking place, "But there's Samson—"

"The concierge allows no animals in the flats. But I'm sure she'll be glad to have him in the courtyard, as added protection for the building. And he'll like having the concierge's children to play with."

"Etienne Perruchot would have to be notified." Not only had I been proposed to by a man who obviously, until half an hour ago, had had no intention of proposing. I also, without putting my acceptance into words, had consented. And in the weird world that was Paris this spring, the whole transaction seemed quite normal.

"I'll get word to him. Drink your Pernod, and then we'll have something to eat.

Our marriage three days later had that same grotesquely matter-of-fact quality. Monsieur Bitzius and Violetta Bernard accompanied us to the office of the district's mayor and signed the necessary papers after the brief ceremony. My employer seemed nonplused, not only by the suddenness with which John and I had decided upon marriage, but by our rejection of his proposal that we have "a little celebration" afterwards.

Monsieur Bitzius and Violetta shook hands with us. Then they turned back toward the ambulance, and John and I walked to the building where he had his flat. In the ground floor hall he said, "Think you can find everything in the kitchen and all?"

I nodded. The concierge, a brisk, no-nonsense woman of about thirty-five, had shown me over the flat that morning. I had also arranged with her that when my trunk came it would be placed in the smaller of the two bedrooms.

"Well, I'd better get to the *Observer* office." He nodded and walked out of the building.

We had not even shaken hands.

Well, what had I expected? Nothing, perhaps. But fool that I was, I had hoped.

I went back to the courtyard to see Samson. Evidently he had understood that the woodshed in one corner was to be his, because I found him lying with his front paws extended across the shed's doorway. To comfort myself as well as him, I patted him and scratched behind his ears. Then I climbed two flights of stairs to my new home.

Chapter 18

During the next few days I caught an occasional glimpse of John. Twice in the early evening we passed each other on the stairs, he going out for dinner, I climbing to that third-floor kitchen to cook my solitary meal. Once, meeting by chance on the street, we walked into the house together and climbed the stairs. But in the top floor hall, he went into the flat by his door, and I by mine.

Twice I was still awake when he came home at night. The wall between my room and the next one was thin enough that I could hear him moving about. Those sounds made me feel lonely—lonelier than I had ever been during those long winter months in the house across the river. Then at least I'd had the hope that someday he might come to me, not to give me some practical gift or bit of advice, but merely because he wanted to see me. Now that hope was gone. Although for some reason he felt responsible for me, so much so that he had given me the protection of his name and his flat, he intended to go on living a life entirely separate from my own.

Until now, when I had lost the hope that he might

turn to me, I had not realized how much it had sustained me. Without it, I felt newly sensitive to the strain of life in this beleaguered city. The suffering around me oppressed me more than at any time in the past, and it was with reluctance that I went to the ambulance each morning.

Five days after that ceremony in the district mayor's office, while I was administering cough syrup to a patient in the ground floor ward, I heard an explosive roar. The floor trembled, and the medicine bottle I had placed on a small stand fell over. A few seconds later a nurse rushed in from the street. An enormous cloud of smoke, she told us, was rising from the western part of the city.

We soon learned why. Whether because of accident or sabotage, a huge arsenal on the Avenue Rapp had blown up. Neighboring houses and shops had been obliterated, and hundreds of people killed or injured. Soon a few of the victims began to arrive at our ambulance. For once the wounded were not soldiers. Most of them were women and children.

I soon saw it would be impossible for me to go home at the usual hour. Aware of tension in the pit of my stomach and a dull ache at the base of my skull, I moved back and forth from the operating room, and up and down the stairs between the wards.

I had just descended to the ground floor about ten o'clock that night when a woman, accompanied by a boy of about fifteen, walked in. She said, "Nurse, can you help me? I am looking for my daughters." Her eyes had an odd brightness, and her lips were curved in an inappropriate smile. "I think they may have been slightly injured in the explosion. Were they brought here?"

"I'll find out. What are their ages?"

"Paulette is ten, and Marie eight. They're both blond, with blue eyes."

"Wait here. All the children are upstairs."

I hurried into the narrow hall between the ward and the operating room, and started toward the stairs. Then, hearing rapid footsteps behind me, I turned around.

It was the boy. "Don't bother to look, nurse. You won't find them. My sisters were out in the garden, and they were—blown up. My mother and I both saw it happen. But now she doesn't remember it, and when I try to remind her, she doesn't even seem to hear me."

His face twisted. "I don't know what to do. We've been going from one place to another for hours now, so she can ask about Paulette and . . ."

Abruptly he turned back into the ward. I leaned my head against the wall and began to cry uncontrollably. I don't know why, after all I'd seen, that I found unbearable the thought of that woman searching for little girls she herself had seen die, but I did.

"All right, you're through for the night." Violetta was standing in front of me. "Go home." I knew that the harshness of her voice was really kindness. "You'll be no good to us here."

A few minutes later, as I hurried down the street, I again began to cry. On the Rue Ramponeau, I was dimly aware of silent, grim-faced women in Guardsmen's uniforms marching up the center of the street. It was the Women's Battalion Charlotte Vinoy had formed, but I did not even try to see if she were with them. I turned one corner, and another, and then I was inside the house on the Rue de Odette. Blinded by tears, I stubbed my toe against the bottom step of the stairs.

160

I was clinging to the newel post, sobbing, when John Lowndes came in from the street. He halted beside me. "Martha! What is it?"

"Nothing. Everything. Oh, just a woman at the ambulance. A woman who's gone crazy—"

"I'll take you to your room."

Arm around my waist, he helped me up the two flights. I tried to unlock the door, but my shaking hand could not find the keyhole. He took the key from me, unlocked the door, and followed me into the room. He said, laying the key on the bureau, "You'd better go straight to bed."

"Don't leave me!" I heard myself saying. I moved toward him. "Please, please! Don't leave me."

His arms went around me. For several moments neither of us spoke. Then he tilted my chin with one hand and looked down at me.

"Don't leave me," I said in a very different tone. I was not crying now.

By the dim glow of the gas jet out in the hall, I saw his face change. He took out his handkerchief and dried my cheeks. Then I felt his hands at the back of my head, taking out the pins. My hair fell down around my shoulders. "There," he said. "That's the way I've always wanted to see you."

He closed the door and came back to me. He said, unbuttoning my jacket, "No, I won't leave you."

Chapter 19

I lay there beside him, in darkness relieved only by dim light from the street lamp far below. My body still ached faintly from love's initiation. And I was happy. It was a novel emotion. I had enjoyed life at intervals during my growing-up years here in Paris, but I had not been happy since those far-off days when both my parents were alive. And my childish content of those days, when I had not known how rare happiness is in this world, seemed pale in comparison with what I felt now.

John said, "I love you." He was looking through the semidarkness at the ceiling.

Turning my head on his shoulder, I burrowed my face into his neck. "And I love you."

"Damned if you don't," he said, stroking my hair, "damned if you don't."

"When did you first know you loved me?"

He said slowly, "I guess it wasn't until tonight that I realized it. But perhaps it started that day we drove out to the Bois de Boulogne. You seemed so touchy and proud and aloof, such a strange girl to be living in Paris these days."

And to be Flora Hathaway's daughter.

I said, "All these months I've wondered if you even liked me. Why did you stay away from me for weeks at a time? Why?"

He said after a moment, "We'll talk about that. Not now, but sometime soon."

"Was it because of Charlotte Vinoy? Tell me if it was. I won't mind, not now." Not with him holding me in his arms.

"No, it wasn't because of Charlotte. I admire her, even though I don't share her ideas. And for a while we wanted each other. But it had nothing to do with love."

"But haven't you ever been in love with anyone?"

He said after a moment's silence, "I thought I was."

"Someone in America?"

"Yes."

"When you came to Paris, did you still think that you were—"

"You talk too much." He had turned his face toward me.

I said, my lips stirring against his, "Yes, I talk too much."

For the next few days I lived in two worlds. One was the world of Paris under the Commune, with its death agonies almost upon it. The Versailles forces held all the high ground to the west now, and rained almost ceaseless fire on the defenders, many of them members of the Women's Battalion, who still held out on the city's fortifications. And hour by hour the Versailles sappers dug their tunnels closer to the walls of Paris.

The other world I lived in had a population of two. Each night I cooked dinner for us in our flat. We talked and talked, but almost never about my day at the ambulance, or the grim dispatches he had sent to the *Observer*, or those men and women out in the streets, building barricades all over Paris of paving stones and barrels and even old furniture. Instead we talked of our separate childhoods, and of where we would live when we returned to New York. And, in the larger of the two bedrooms, which was now mine as well as his, we made love.

One night, lying beside him, I said, "It's very selfish of us, isn't it? Being happy, making love, when all around us—"

"No, it's quite natural. You know about Vesuvius, don't you?"

"Just that it erupted."

"Yes, and the night after it did, when thousands still lay buried under the lava, the fields around Naples were filled with couples like us."

I said after a moment, "You mean it is nature striking a balance? Trying to insure that even though thousands die—"

"Something like that, perhaps. Anyway, that was what happened."

Chapter 20

Before eight the next day, John and I said goodbye on the doorstep and then walked off in opposite directions, he toward the *Observer* offices, I toward the ambulance. I had just turned the corner when I saw Etienne Perruchot moving toward me through the crowd of work-bound Parisians. He stopped and said, with a formal little bow, "Good day, Madame Lowndes." His brown eyes, although serious, held none of the anger I had seen there at our last meeting.

I said, "Good day, monsieur. What brings you to this neighborhood?"

"My hatmaker. His shop is on this street."

I hesitated and then said, "I hope you were able to find a caretaker."

He flushed, obviously remembering those final words of his at our last meeting. "Not yet. In the meantime the police of the district are keeping a close watch." He paused. "Madame—"

"Yes, monsieur?"

"I am sorry that I—wounded your quite natural feelings about your mother that day. I was clumsy. But I was trying to—to define the situation as I saw it."

I thought of how John had said, "He was being honest." I smiled at him. Basically he was a very nice person, this handsome, overserious young man. I found myself liking him better than at any time in the past. I said, "I too was not very kind that day."

"We were both overwrought." He hesitated, and then said with a rush, "But the other sentiments I expressed that day—they were sincere, madame. Since you are married now, I realize it is unlikely that you will ever need me in any way. But I hope that if you do, you will turn to me."

I said, meaning it, "I will, monsieur."

"Well, I had best get to my hatter's while there is still time."

"Time?"

"You have not heard? Government soldiers entered the city last night. They just walked in. The foolish rebels left one of the western gates unguarded. They say most of Passy is already in government hands."

My face must have betrayed what I felt, because he added, "I am sorry to be the one to tell you. You are concerned, of course, for the welfare of the people among whom you work. Even though I don't share those sympathies, I understand them. Well, goodbye, madame."

I hurried on, aware now of tension in the faces of people I passed. But no street corner speakers harangued crowds. In fact, the streets were quieter than usual.

At the ambulance I found that same unnatural calm. Both staff and patients had the grim, quiet air of those who know they are doomed, but intend to go down fighting. Monsieur Bitzius, who on other days visited the ambulance briefly or not at all, remained in his office.

166

Perhaps he was preparing records to give to whatever new authority demanded them. Now and then people came in with news. The Versailles forces held all the western part of the city now, and moved, despite the desperate men firing from behind barricades, toward the heart of Paris—the Place de la Concorde, and the Place Vendôme, and that street, the Rue de Rivoli, which led straight to the Hôtel de Ville and its wrangling, speech-making occupants.

Shortly after six, I hurried home. Now I could hear the distant rattle of rifle fire and the deep boom of cannon. But even so, in this limpid May air, this crystalline light of early evening, it was difficult to realize that Frenchmen were fighting each other inside their beautiful city with far more savagery than any of them had ever turned against the Prussians.

It was past eight when John came into the flat, looking tired. Loath to hear details, I merely asked, "How long do you think it will last?"

"It's hard to say. So far the Versailles forces have been fighting in neighborhoods friendly to them. It will be a different story here in the eastern part of Paris."

At dinner he said, after we had eaten in silence for several minutes, "I have to be out on the streets. It's my job. But you had best stay in the flat from now on."

"I can't. I can't desert sick people dependent upon me."

It was more than that. I had learned something about myself that day. Oh, I still knew that the Commune leaders were a group of pompous incompetents. I still felt disgusted and angered by the widespread drunkenness in the National Guard. But now, when the crisis was here, I had learned that whatever sympathies I had in this struggle in a country not my own lay with the people among whom I worked each day. Those gaunt housewives, anxiously counting their centimes outside a shop before they went in to buy a few ounces of horse-meat. Their husbands, hoping for a life that would hold more than moldering slums, undersized children, and temporary oblivion in wineshops. And all those men, women, and children who, after the Commune was declared a few weeks before, had wandered through the parks and splendid squares of their city with that look of dreamy delight in their eyes.

John argued with me for several minutes. Then he said, sighing, "A tornado, a balky mule, and a stubborn woman. All right. It won't be really dangerous until the fighting spreads to this part of the city. And that should take several days."

It took four days—terrible days during which the Communards, fighting for their very lives now, fell back from barricade to barricade. Days in which the sound of gunfire, drawing ever closer, became so constant that I, hurrying from ward to ward, was no longer really aware of it, until some louder sound, such as the earth-rocking explosion of a second arsenal, this time on the Left Bank, made me freshly conscious of noise. Days in which each hour seemed to bring news of some new atrocity and counter-atrocity. Versailles soldiers had broken into an ambulance in the western part of the city and, despite the pleas of the English doctor in charge, had shot wounded National Guardsmen where they lay. And lieutenants of the unspeakable Rigault had taken the aged archbishop and five other clerics from their cells and shot them to death.

By Thursday a pall of smoke hung over the city. The

168

Communards as they fell back had put to the torch that splendid Tuileries Palace from which Empress Eugénie had fled last September. Other fires blazed along the Rue de Rivoli, and on the Left Bank. No one seemed to know whether they had been set deliberately, or were the result of cannon fire, or such explosions as that of the Left Bank arsenal not far from Etienne Perruchot's house.

Late that afternoon Violetta Bernard called all the nurses together in that top floor room set aside for us. There would be fighting in this neighborhood soon, she said. "During the next few hours we will instruct patients who can move about, so that they can give the bedridden at least a little care. After that you are to go to your homes and stay there. Monsieur Bitzius and I will stay here at the ambulance."

When someone protested that some of the critically ill patients might die, she said, "We feel that all of them will be safer if this place remains as inconspicuous as possible, with the shades drawn and the door locked, and no staff members moving in and out."

No need to ask what she meant. We had more than a score of wounded National Guardsmen in that ground floor ward. If Versailles soldiers had invaded that other ambulance, they might be even less inclined toward mercy here in the Communard stronghold of Belleville.

Hours later the wounded men in the two rows of beds on the ground floor watched us go. Some wished us good luck, and one young Guardsman, who'd had an ear shot away, called out, "Get home safe, my pretties. I intend to call on each and every one of you after I'm out of here." But most of them were silent. I glanced swiftly at each face as I moved along the aisle. They did not look frightened or apathetic, but merely stoical. Perhaps a consistently unlucky gambler, turning away from the table where he has lost his last cent, has that look on his face.

At the corner I saw that people of the neighborhood were building a barricade across Rue Ramponeau. They worked swiftly and in almost complete silence, the men heaving pavement blocks into place, women rolling barrels out the doorway of a wineshop, and children staggering under the weight of wooden boxes and rickety chairs. I hurried on through air acrid with smoke. Now and then blackened bits of paper rained down. Perhaps archives were burning somewhere, those enormous archives of French officialdom, and the blackened scraps I brushed from my face were part of someone's tax statement or marriage license.

When I reached the house on Rue de Odette, I went back along the hall to the courtyard to see Samson, and to make sure that the concierge's children, who insisted upon giving him his dinner, had not forgotten to do so tonight. Apparently the gunfire and the smoke-laden air had upset him, because he had left most of his dinner uneaten, and when he came out of the shed, he pressed against my legs, whining, as if to plead that I take him upstairs with me. I soothed and petted him. At my urging, he ate the rest of the food in his dish, and then padded back into the shed.

I found the flat empty. Had John had dinner? Probably not, anymore than I had. I was in the kitchen, wondering whether to make a soufflé that might or might not fall before he came home, when someone knocked at the hall door.

It was the concierge. "There's a man downstairs who

demands to see the identity cards of all the people in the house."

"Identity cards!"

"Yes, madame. You know how about two weeks ago the Commune issued everyone an identity card."

"Yes, of course. But I shouldn't think that *now*—"

"You know how they are."

Yes, I knew how they were, those Frenchmen on the lowest rungs of the civil service. While regimes came and went, they continued their tasks with the efficiency of automatons. Perhaps days ago, before the Versailles troops had streamed through that unguarded gate, some superior of this man's had passed down the order that identity cards were to be checked. No one had thought to countermand the order. And so now, with the city burning in a score of places and rifle bullets whining through the streets, he plodded from house to house, demanding identity cards.

"Mine is in my reticule. I don't know where my husband's is, but probably it is here." I recalled his remarking two days before that in neighborhoods held by the Versailles troops, his *Observer* card was far greater protection than one issued by the Commune.

"Please try to find both cards, madame. And hurry. If that man downstairs should make a fuss, a crowd might gather. And if someone gets the notion that there is a spy in this house—well, you know what might happen."

Yes, I knew only too well. "I'll hurry," I said, and closed the door.

His card was not on his bureau. I opened the top drawer and gingerly moved aside the pistol that lay there atop a pile of clippings he had made from Paris newspapers. Only two nights before, remarking that in times like these it was best to be prepared for the worst, John had showed me how to use that gun, in case someone tried to break into the flat while I was alone here. The identity card was not in that drawer, nor in any of the others.

Opening the wardrobe, I looked vainly through the pockets of two of his suits. I hauled down an empty valise resting on the lower wardrobe shelf, and searched its various compartments. No card. Perhaps it had fallen from some pocket onto the wardrobe floor. Kneeling, I not only inspected the floor, but turned two pairs of his shoes upside-down and shook them.

There was only one place left to look—the top wardrobe shelf. It appeared to be empty, but then, it was more than a foot higher than my head, and so I could not be sure. If it were not there, John must have it with him. I would have to go downstairs and explain as best I could to that man who, however dry and plodding, was potentially dangerous.

Getting to my feet, I stood on tiptoe and felt along the shelf. My fingers encountered what felt like the edge of a shallow cardboard box. Stretching even farther, I drew it to the shelf's edge and started to lift it down. But I had been unable to grasp it firmly enough. The bottom half of the box fell out, spilling sheets of paper onto the floor, and a photograph in a small mother-of-pearl frame.

The picture had landed face up. I stood there with the boxtop in my hand, looking down at that photograph. Even though more than seven years had passed since the last time I had seen that pictured face, I recognized it. The girl was Laura Hathaway, my father's young sister. Laura, that lovely blonde I had never called Aunt Laura, because she was only six years older than myself.

Chapter 21

I bent over and picked up the photograph in its pretty frame. The pictured face appeared to be that of a woman in her early twenties. No, she would be around twenty-seven now. But apparently she was even more attractive now than she had been at nineteen. The spoiled look she'd once had—the expression my mother called "Laura's snippy look"—had given way to the poised graciousness of a woman sure of her beauty and its power.

There was an inscription written in a flowing hand: "For John from Laura, with fond affection."

Not once in all the months I had known him had he hinted at even the slightest acquaintance with my father's family.

My heart had begun to pound. And a word had begun to pound over and over in my brain. Liar, liar, liar. I placed the photograph face down on the bureau. I knelt, and with hands that felt cold began to gather up the scattered sheets of paper. Obviously they were parts of two letters, one written with heavy pressure in a small, crabbed hand, the other in the same graceful script that was on the photograph.

174

I sat down in the armchair near the bed and began to sort the pages. As I did so, I tried not to read sentences or even phrases. I knew I must proceed in an orderly fashion, lest my sense of betrayal overwhelm me. When I had the pages sorted, I laid Laura's letter aside on the bedside stand.

According to its heading, the other letter had been written in New York, on the fifth of the previous June. The salutation was, "My dear John." Turning to the last page, I saw that the letter had been signed by James Hathaway.

My father's younger brother, my Uncle James. I might have called him that, since he was several years older than his sister. But I never had called him anything, for the simple reason that we had never met. My closest view of him had been the one afforded me that day when I looked out the window of that Washington Square flat and saw him waiting, spine ramrod-stiff, blond hair bright in the sunlight, in the carriage three stories below.

James Hathaway had written: "It was good indeed to get your letter, with its report on the woman my poor misguided brother married—although as you know, in my opinion and that of my late father, it was no marriage at all. Unfortunately, my dear mother is less firm in her convictions, and allows her heart to rule not only her head but her religious principles.

"But to return to the information in your letter. Family friends over the past five years have brought back stories about Flora Hathaway and the man who keeps her. My mother has steadily refused to believe them. Although her stroke of five years ago has impaired her speech and her use of her limbs, it has done nothing to lessen her stubborn attachment to that woman and her child. She keeps insisting that she knows Flora Hathaway is supporting herself as an actress, because she herself saw the contract!"

For a moment I stared unseeingly at the wall. A stroke. That was why my grandmother had not replied to either of the letters my mother had sent her. She had been unable to reply. I lowered my gaze and went on reading.

"Sometimes I think it would have been mercy, not only to my mother but to Laura and me, if God had seen fit to gather her unto Himself five years ago. As it is she lies there, impaired both in body and mind. I am sure that her mind is impaired, and that therefore that monstrous will she has drawn up should have no legal standing. But it will have, thanks to her doctor and lawyer—both lifelong friends of hers—who insist that although her speech is thick, her mind is as clear as ever. It is outrageous beyond words. Here she plans to leave half the money my father gathered over a lifetime—half, mind you!—to that wanton woman and to the child my mother persists in calling her granddaughter.

"As I am sure you will agree once you catch even a glimpse of the girl, she could scarcely be of Hathaway blood. Quite obviously, she is the product of some earlier adulterous connection of her mother's. As you can realize, the calling my poor brother chose often necessitated his traveling with various road companies, leaving his wife alone in New York."

Rage blurred my vision and made my hands shake until the crisp pages rattled. I closed my eyes, thinking of all the times when—walking with my parents through Washington Square or past the cages at the zoo, or just sitting with them at the dinner table—I had felt warm and safe and happy, not only because they loved me, but because I knew they loved each other.

After a while I was able to go on reading. "But perhaps now we can convince my mother, aided by the factual evidence in your letter. Trust a journalist to gather details! That Flora Hathaway never appeared on a Paris stage, for instance, and that this Perruchot is frequently seen entering a shop whose rear wall adjoins that of a house he owns, and which she occupies."

Again my fury made the words blur. I waited a moment, and then went on reading. "It is unfortunate that you have not yet caught a glimpse of Flora Hathaway's daughter. If she is still at that convent school, perhaps you could see her there. I am sure that you, as a journalist, could contrive some plausible excuse for visiting the school.

"In the meantime, your letter will go far toward preventing a tenderhearted and therefore easily deceived woman from perpetrating a terrible injustice. She likes you, John. Your letter will carry weight with her. And when she again sees you in person—and may that be soon!—surely you can convince her beyond any doubt that she has been deceived all these years.

"You are being a true friend to Laura and me in this unhappy matter. Although I hesitate to mention it, I hope that your stake in its outcome will be more than that of a friend. It is with pleasure that I have watched the growing attachment between you and my sister. There are religious differences, of course, but I gather you have no heartfelt convictions which would stand in the way of resolving that problem. In short, my dear John, even though I realize that it is up to you and Laura to decide when that happy day will arrive, I already look forward to calling you brother-in-law.

177

"Although your letter was addressed to us both, Laura is sending a separate reply."

I stared at James Hathaway's signature for a moment. Then I folded the pages carefully together and laid them on the stand. Don't try to think yet, I warned myself. Read her letter first.

It was much shorter than her brother's. She had addressed him as "Dear John," and then written:

"How grateful we are for your letter. We have not read it yet to Mama. First we must decide how to do it as tactfully as possible, so that the shock to the poor darling will be no greater than necessary.

"John, I know what an unpleasant task we set for you. True, you realized it was necessary for all our sakes, including poor Mama's. Still, it must be distasteful. And so please don't feel that you must *talk* to either of those two. In fact, I would be very distressed to learn that you had done so, because I would know how much you had hated it. Anyway, just looking at them—especially Martha!—should be enough.

"Although I can feel no sympathy for her mother, I do feel sorry for Martha, and not just because of the sordidness of her present circumstances. Even when we were both children—I'm a bit older than her, you know—I used to feel sorry for her. She was such a dark, scrawny little thing, with none of her mother's looks, and of course none of the Hathaway's!

"Oh, dear! How vain that sounds, and I did not mean it that way at all. But I was pleased to read in your letter that you often look at that photograph you asked for before you left. Perhaps, even with all those Parisian beauties about, you will not forget me.

She had signed herself, "Your affectionate Laura."

I sat motionless, the letter in my lap. He had "looked" at us, all right. In my mind's eye I again saw him, staring upward at that theater box. But he had done more than look. He had come to the box, claimed acquaintanceship with Marcel Ranier—liar, liar!—and thus contrived to be introduced to my mother and me.

Why? Was it in pursuit of some plan to make absolutely sure that my mother and I inherited nothing from that stroke-crippled but stubborn woman in New York?

Certainly my mother would inherit nothing now.

I thought of a shadowy figure crossing the courtyard the night of my mother's death, and tapping on the window glass until she looked out. She must have seen someone she knew and trusted. Otherwise she would not have opened the door.

She would have opened it to John Lowndes. She had been so eager, my poor mother, to find a husband for me . . .

I put the heels of my hands against my temples. From somewhere not too far away came the rattle of rifle fire. Just because the whole world had gone crazy was no reason that I should. And they were crazy, these thoughts tumbling through my head. John loved me. And I loved him. I had loved him since the second time I saw him.

But was it really John Lowndes I had loved? No, because until tonight I had not even known him. Certainly I never would have loved him if I'd had any knowledge of these letters.

And yet he had married me, even if his only reason had been to insure my safety.

Or to insure its opposite.

The thought held me cold, motionless. He had known

—everyone had known—that soon the Communards and the Versailles forces would be locked in bloody struggle here inside the city. Who would stop even to wonder about a young woman shot to death in a doorway, or on some dark street?

My mother was dead. I was not—not yet.

A childish phrase leaped into my mind. One down, one to go.

That was insane. He loved me. Night after night we had lain in each other's arms here on this very bed. He loved me.

But more than one woman, married to a man she scarcely knew, had died by his hand soon after the ceremony. Had those women—until they faced the leveled gun, the drawn knife—believed that they were beloved?

A memory flashed through my mind. John at that Christmas Eve party. Just before nausea overwhelmed me, he had said something about a two-headed lamb.

My mother, desperation in her dying face, had tried to tell me something about a two-headed sheep.

I had a sense that the walls were moving closer together, threatening to crush me. I had to get out of here before he came back. But where could I go?

There was a police station not two hundred yards away. But when I passed it on my way to the flat, it had been dark and shuttered. Probably all of the stations in this area were. The police, who hundreds of times this past terrible year had clashed with the unruly National Guard, would be out in the streets now, fighting on the side of the Versailles soldiers.

The ambulance. I would go there. I would make them let me in.

Hands clumsy in their haste, I assembled the letters

and the photograph and placed them in their shallow box. Had the photograph been on top before? I could not know. The box had spilled its contents while I was taking it down. I thrust the box as far back as I could on the top wardrobe shelf. Then I left the flat and ran down two flights of stairs.

In the ground floor hall I almost collided with the concierge. "Oh, Madame Lowndes! I should have come up to tell you. He's gone." She must have seen the incomprehension in my face, because she added, "The man who was checking identity cards. Three Guardsmen came and took him away to help build barricades."

"Oh," I said, and moved toward the front door.

"Madame Lowndes! Where are you going?"

I turned. "I'm going out."

"But it is not safe! And what shall I tell your husband when he comes?"

"Tell him I went out." I opened the door, closed it behind me, and ran down the steps.

Chapter 22

Before I even reached the corner, I realized that I should have tried to think of some excuse for leaving the house. When the concierge told John Lowndes how I had dashed out, looking distraught and giving no explanation whatever, he might conclude that I had found that box on the wardrobe shelf. Whether he did or not, he almost surely would guess that I had gone to the ambulance. Well, it was too late now.

Soon after I turned the corner, I saw four Guardsmen and two women in Guardsmen's uniforms running toward me, rifles held loosely in their hands, faces grim in the glow of the fires burning along the river. I don't think they even saw me. As I moved on, aware of crackling rifle fire not far away, and of that silent rain of charred paper, I passed two more groups of silently running Guardsmen. Otherwise the streets were deserted. No, not quite. In the Rue Ramponeau those elderly men, women and children still worked on the barricade. It was higher now, well above the top of a tall man's head. I turned onto the upward sloping side street, ran about a hundred yards, and hammered on the ambulance's closed door.

"It's Martha! Let me in!"

After a while Violetta opened the door, her long face stern. "What are you doing here? I told you—"

"I had to come. I have to see Monsieur Bitzius."

Muttering under her breath, she let me in. I heard her lock the door behind me. As I moved along the aisle between the beds, none of the patients spoke to me, although I sensed that each of them was tensely awake.

When I entered Monsieur Bitzius's office, I found him seated at his desk. His face, turning toward me, looked startled. "Child! What is it?" Then, as I started to speak: "No, sit down first. Catch your breath."

A few moments later he said, "All right. Now tell me."

I did, helplessly aware that my account was half incoherent, with the events out of sequence. The photograph and the two letters. My mother's last, confused words, and the strange remark John Lowndes had made at the Christmas party. The lie by which he had gained admittance to the theater box. Then back to the letters.

At last Monsieur Bitzius said, "I can see how you would be very hurt and angry, Martha. He deceived you and your mother from what must seem to you very shabby motives. What's more, he kept silent about it even after he married you. But don't you see that probably he was ashamed to tell you?

"And anyway," he went on, "there's a great deal of difference between deception and murder. Can you really believe he killed your mother, and now intends to kill you? Martha, you have lived with this man. And you have been happy. You have had the look of a young woman who not only loves a man, but is sure that he loves her. In this dismal place, it has been a pleasure just to look at you."

"Yes," I said bitterly, "I was very sure."

"And you haven't yet given me any clear reason why he should have wanted your mother to die, or you either."

"The Hathaway money. With both my mother and me out of the way, he could marry Laura—"

"Oh, yes. That young aunt of yours. Don't you see that there is no evidence that he's even been in touch with her for many months now? Something must have happened that caused him to put her out of his mind, so completely that he even forgot about that photograph and those letters."

Even though I did not say so, I found that unconvincing. If something had happened to turn him against Laura, he would have destroyed her photograph or returned it to her. He would not have preserved it carefully on that wardrobe shelf, along with her letter and her brother's.

I said, "I can see that you think I am just hysterical."

His voice was dry. "Yes. But in a city which has manifested every sort of hysteria for many months now, why should you be the exception? Now go home. Tomorrow morning you and I will discuss this matter calmly, and decide what is to be done. Don't go up to your flat if you are still afraid of him. Ask the concierge to let you stay in her flat tonight."

Of course. Why hadn't I thought of that before I dashed into the streets?

"And you had better go soon. From what I have heard, the whole Left Bank is now in Versailles hands, and most of the Right Bank along the river front. The Communards will be falling back to man the barricades here in Belleville. So go now, while you still can."

184

I left him. In the little vestibule, Violetta opened the door. I heard her lock and bar it behind me. Moments later I saw that the Rue Ramponeau was now deserted. The old men and women and children, their grim task complete, now waited behind locked doors for whatever the night would bring. Aware of that constant crackle of gunfire, I turned onto another street, stretching emptily away under the gaslight, and then onto another.

Fifty or more Guardsmen were running toward me up the center of the street. So already they were falling back upon Belleville. I saw several of them turn, send rifle fire down the street, and then, turning back, run to catch up with their companions. Instinctively I flattened myself against a building's stone wall.

"Martha!"

John stood on the opposite curb, his face white and contorted by some violent emotion. Fear? Rage?

All the terror that Monsieur Bitzius had dispelled only partially came flooding back. Again I had that vision of John Lowndes tapping at the window, saw my mother smiling at him through the glass, and then hurrying to the door to let him in. I thought of him, only minutes ago, discovering the disarranged contents of that box, and then leaving the flat with that pistol under his coat —the pistol that I, in my pain and anger and fear, had not thought to take with me. And I pictured myself lying dead in one of these streets, a victim of a stray Versailles bullet, or one fired by a Communard. Who would even bother to wonder which it had been?

The retreating men had swept between us. My blood drumming in my ears, I ran on down the street, turned onto another. After a few yards I came to a deep door-way. I turned into it and, in the darkness, pressed close to one of its side walls. Had he caught a glimpse of me turning into this street?

I could still hear rifle fire on the street I had just left, but it sounded more distant now. I cowered against the wall, not even trying to think, just drawing air deep into my lungs and waiting for my heartbeats to slow. Then, in the comparative silence, I heard the pound of a man's running feet.

I caught a glimpse of him as he ran past the doorway. Had he thrown a glance into its darkness? If so, he had failed to see me. The sound of his footsteps faded. Should I leave this temporary hiding place, go to that house on Rue de Odette and seek shelter until morning behind the concierge's locked door? Instantly I rejected the idea. I did not want to go anywhere near that house and that third-floor flat. And anyway, he might intercept me before I got there.

A moment later I was glad I had not moved from that deep doorway. I heard his returning footsteps, this time along the other side of the street. I moved from the wall to stand with my back to the building's door, so that I had a view of the opposite sidewalk. I saw him run past. Moving to the doorway's other wall, I watched him turn the corner. Apparently he had decided that I had not gone down this street after all, but had continued along the one where we had stared at each other from opposite sidewalks.

I waited until I could hear nothing but distant rifle fire. Then I turned, pounded on the door, and called, "Please! Let me in!"

There was no response, but then, I had not expected any. With civil war raging in the streets, it would be only an exceptionally foolhardy person, or an exceptionally compassionate one, who would open his door to a stranger tonight.

I leaned my cheek against the door's solid wooden panel and tried to think. Should I just stay here until daylight? No, when he did not find me elsewhere, he might decide to search this street again, and more carefully.

Suddenly I thought of that house off the Boulevard Saint-Germain, where I had waged my winter-long battle against cold, hunger, and loneliness. Surely that house, perhaps two miles away across battle-torn Paris, was the last place he would look for me.

And if the entire Left Bank and the Right Bank close to the river were now in Versailles hands, it meant that fighting had ceased there. Once I reached the river, I would be comparatively safe. And the river was not far. If I were very careful, if I moved from one doorway shelter to another, and made sure before I turned into any street that I could see no barricade, or armed, scurrying men . . .

I waited for a few moments more, drawing air deep into my lungs. Then I moved to the doorway entrance. When I was sure that the street lay deserted in both directions, I turned to my left and hurried away.

Chapter 23

I lost all track of time that night. Again and again, after turning into what seemed a deserted street, I saw running Guardsmen emerge from a side street, and had to dodge into a doorway. One time there were men in the uniform of Breton Mobiles, those arch enemies of the Communards, in close pursuit, firing as they ran. I waited until the sound of their rifles had faded into the distance before I moved on.

I was not the only noncombatant out in the streets that terrible night. Several times, turning a corner, I caught a glimpse of a shadowy, hurrying figure in civilian clothes. Twice it was a woman. Each time, long before I could catch up to ask for shelter, he or she turned into a building, leaving me only the sound of a slammed door and turning locks. In some part of my mind not completely absorbed by my own peril, I wondered how it was that these people, too, had been out in the streets. Had that last woman, for instance, been hurrying home from the bedside of some desperately ill loved one?

More than once I started around a corner and then quickly drew back, because there was a barricade down there, its defenders darkly silhouetted against the pulsing glow of fires along the river. I had a growing sense of nightmarish unreality. Had I really seen those letters addressed to my husband, the husband I had loved so passionately, or had I just dreamed it? If I had, then it was still only in a dream that I moved through this city that was not my own, this city where flame reflections wavered along stone house fronts and rifle fire reverberated in the streets. Perhaps soon I would awake with a strangled cry, and John would take me in his arms and speak soothing words until the nightmare faded.

But I knew that such thoughts came to me only because I so wished that it was in a dream that I moved through the dark streets, sometimes forced to retrace my steps, but gradually drawing near the Seine. I had long since lost a sense of exactly where I was, but I was sure that my circuitous route had taken me farther east than I had planned.

What time was it? One in the morning? Two? I had no idea. I only knew that for at least fifteen minutes I had seen no armed men of any kind. And the last three barricades I had glimpsed as I hurried across intersections stood dark and silent, deserted now by the men who had defended them.

Finally I emerged onto a wide street and, looking to my right, saw how far east I had come. Down there was the Hôtel de Ville, facing its wide square. And it was on fire, its flames rising almost straight up in the windless air. Where were they now, all those Communard leaders who for two months had wrangled day after day in that stately medieval pile?

There seemed to be lots of activity down there. I saw the brassy gleam of fire engines, and the restless movements of the horses hitched to them. I also saw human figures scurrying about, dark in that fiery light. But there was no sound of gunfire. And only a few yards beyond that flaming structure was a bridge. I could cross it to the island which supported Notre Dame's dark bulk, and then cross another bridge to the Left Bank.

Keeping far to the right side of the square in front of the flaming structure, I hurried forward. Not only firemen fought the blaze, I saw now. Uniformed army men helped man the pumps and hold the fire hoses.

A hand caught my arm. Heart leaping with terror, I felt myself spun around. But it was a man of about thirty-five in a sergeant's uniform who stood there scowling at me. "Where are you going?"

I said, past the pulse pounding in my throat, "To my house."

"Let me see your hands, palms up."

Bewildered, I held out my hands. He looked at them, and then bent low over my palms, sniffing.

"What is all this, Sergeant?"

I looked up and saw a younger man in a captain's uniform. Straightening, the sergeant said, "This girl. I thought she might have been firing a rifle or throwing bottles of petroleum."

I understood then. When rifles used by the National Guard were fired, they left smudges on the fingers. At the ambulance it had been said that Versailles troops were shooting anyone, man or woman, found with smudged fingers. And a number of women suspected of throwing "fire balls"—flaming bottles of petroleum—into ground floor windows had been executed. Several of them, according to rumor, had been old women returning empty milk bottles to shops.

190

"Well, have you found any sign of petroleum or of nitrate smudges on her hands?"

"No, sir."

"Then get back to that pump. Now, mademoiselle, why are you here at this hour of the morning?"

"I'm trying to get to my house." I gave him the street number. Would that explanation satisfy him?

Apparently it did, perhaps because he had more important matters on hand than questioning an unarmed young woman. "All right. Go on."

As I moved onto the quay, I saw a squad of Breton Mobiles coming toward me across the bridge. They did not move, tense-faced and crouching, like their comrades I had seen in still-disputed territory. They sang as they marched, and on their faces, made ruddy by the flames of the burning City Hall, was the triumphant look I had seen on the faces of the Prussians as they marched into Paris.

Standing to one side, I waited until the last of them had reached the quay. Then I hurried across the bridge and moved past Notre Dame's mighty facade. Fleetingly I remembered hearing that extreme anti-clericals like Rigault had planned to burn the cathedral if Versailles forces entered the city. Weary and heartsick as I was, I still felt glad that something or someone had stayed their hands. I crossed to the Left Bank, and soon was moving down Boulevard Saint-Germain.

At least along this stretch, the boulevard was so quiet that almost one might have thought that no war raged within a hundred miles. If days or hours ago barricades had stretched across the street, all traces of them had been removed. And in front of a darkened shop a stout woman, with that Parisian facility for turning to the concerns of everyday life as soon as a convulsion of violence has passed, calmly swept broken glass into the gutter.

As I turned off the boulevard into that familiar street, I suddenly remembered that Etienne Perruchot had mentioned that the police were keeping a "close watch" on his house. But of course no policeman stood at the courtyard gate now, or even lingered nearby. Still, I could not get into the house by way of the courtyard. Even if I had brought my reticule with me, which I had not, I would not have been able to unlock the front door. Before that morning ceremony in the mayor's office, I had given the key to this house to John, so that he could return it to Etienne Perruchot.

I went down the narrow alley and descended areaway steps to the window which someone, last Christmas Eve, had broken to gain entrance to the house. None of its panes had been broken since. I slipped off my left shoe. With its heel I struck the same pane that other intruder had broken, and heard the tinkle of glass on the kitchen floor. When I had replaced my shoe, I reached carefully inside the jagged opening and turned the latch. I had to push hard against the sash, but finally the lower half of the window rose. I saw down on the areaway's pavement, swung my legs over the sill, and then slid down into the darkened house.

Chapter 24

When I had closed and latched the window, I turned around. Dim light from the gas lamp at the alley's entrance filtered into the kitchen. I could make out the table from which I had eaten so many solitary meals, but not the wooden box of matches which always had rested on it. My groping hands found the box, struck a light. There on the wooden sinkboard, just where I had left it, was the oil lamp with its brass base and its tall chimney of frosted glass.

With the lighted lamp in my hand, I climbed steps to the ground floor, and moved along the hall to the library. It, too, was just as I had left it, with the ashes of the last fire I had kindled still in the grate. Probably Etienne Perruchot had briefly inspected this house after John Lowndes returned the key to him. But it looked to me as if otherwise it had stood here empty and undisturbed.

I turned, looked at the salon's closed door, and then, with the reluctance which always weighted my steps when I was about to enter the room where my mother had died, I crossed the hall. I opened the door and then stopped short, feeling stunned. Despite the familiar aspect of the kitchen and library, I was convinced for several seconds that I had entered the wrong house.

The salon's opposite wall, with its richly carved panels, simply had disappeared. In its place was a steeply pitched staircase leading up to a platform, set perhaps six feet below the room's lofty ceiling. The platform was narrow, only a foot or so wider than the single bed, a canopied four-poster, which stood upon it. Even from the doorway, and with no illumination except that from the oil lamp in my hand, I could see that the bed's dark red hangings were in tatters.

After several bewildered seconds I realized that the carved wall panels had not disappeared, after all. They merely had collapsed. Some lengths, their plain sides exposed now, lay flat on the floor. Others stood at an angle, propped up by furniture. One length, which evidently had struck the marble mantel as it descended, now lay on one edge, screening the fireplace opening.

The explosion of that Left Bank arsenal only the day before? Yes, that must have done it, although perhaps the wall had been weakened earlier when that Prussian shell plunged through the skylight.

Strange to stand here, in a Paris only three decades away from the twentieth century, and look at that platform. But I knew that such concealed rooms had been fairly common two or three hundred years ago or more. Then most wars had been fought, not even between nations, let alone classes, but between ambitious nobles, many of them rich enough, and far-sighted enough, to build such hiding places for themselves or their hard-pressed adherents. And in the thick-walled houses built here, in one of the most ancient parts of Paris, concealing such a narrow room as that one up there had been a simple matter.

194

Carrying the lamp, I moved farther into the wreckage-strewn salon. A length of paneling, which had collapsed onto a sofa and a small table near the long windows, blocked my way to the foot of those stairs. I set down the lamp, and with both hands tilted the panel until, flopping over in midair, it fell flat on the floor. I picked up the lamp and moved on.

My foot struck a small fragment of wood. I paused and looked down at it. A carved fleur-de-lis, and part of the carved garland of vine leaves which had encircled it. The wall's intricate pattern had included scores of fleurs-de-lis, each surrounded by garlands of fruit, flowers, or vine leaves.

My mother, as she lay there on a Savonnerie carpet now covered by the wrecked wall, had not only talked of a two-headed sheep. She also, with that despairing urgency in her eyes, had said something about a fleur-de-lis. Had she been struggling to tell me of one particular fleur-de-lis among all of those on that wall, one marking the site of a concealed spring which, when pressed, would open the entrance to that staircase? I moved on and, with my pulses beating fast, climbed to the platform.

Once a carpet, probably a fine one, had covered these boards. Time had eaten ragged holes in it and reduced the areas that held the holes together to the bare threads. I looked at the bed. Most of the nap was gone from its red velvet covering. How long since anyone had slept in that bed? Two hundred years? More?

A round commode stood at the bed's foot, perhaps with a *pot de chambre* still concealed by its curved door. It looked sturdy enough. I set the lamp down on it.

It was not until then that I noticed a convex wooden

shield, oval in shape, hanging there on the bare stone wall perhaps two feet beyond the foot of the bed. It was the kind of gilded and painted shield which still ornamented the gates or doorways of some splendid old Paris houses.

Against the gilded background, a field of purple clover. And superimposed on the field, a white sheep with two heads in profile, each with a glaring yellow eye and curved golden horns. One of its forefeet was raised, as if to rake a sharp golden hoof down the viewer's face.

Something behind the shield?

For perhaps half a minute I stood there, somehow afraid to learn the answer. The lamp flickered, and that grotesque animal seemed to move, almost as if preparing to lash out at me with that sharp hoof. There must be a draught from somewhere. Again the lamp flickered, and this time I felt a faint stir of air. I looked up. Three round holes in the ceiling of the platform. Ventilation pipes, running to the roof?

I looked back at the shield. It was only a wooden emblem. Reaching out, I tipped its lower edge away from the wall.

A folded sheet of paper slid down the wall with a dry, rustling sound and landed on that rotting carpet. I forced myself to bend, pick up the paper, and unfold it.

Just an ordinary sheet of paper, covered with numbers and letters and mathematical symbols.

I remembered Professor Richard's distraught old face, there on the darkened street corner. Had I found a paper, he had asked, with numbers and symbols on it? When I had asked him what sort of paper it was, he had taken refuge in loftiness. "That is a scientific matter, and beyond your comprehension."

He had been right about that. But one thing was clear to me. Those incomprehensible numbers and symbols had been important to my mother, too. No need to wonder in what way. For her this sheet of paper must have meant money. "Take it to him," she had said, and I had thought, and still thought, that she must have meant Frederick Mosser, he of the limp and the gallant manner. She must have had reason to think he would pay well for this piece of paper in my hand. Perhaps he was still willing to pay for it.

And my poor mother had not only known she was dying. She had known that her daughter—her stiff-necked daughter, no doubt headed for spinsterhood—would be left alone and penniless.

Again the lamp flickered. Those numbers and symbols seemed to squirm on the page, as if possessed of some evil life of their own. I had an almost irresistible impulse to turn and hold the paper above the lamp chimney until it turned brown and then burst into flames. But because of this paper—I was sure of it—my mother had died. I must not destroy something that might reveal the person who had taken her life.

A grating sound. I turned swiftly to face the salon doorway and then stood motionless. Someone was turning a key in the front door lock. Etienne Perruchot? Then, with the pulse leaping almost painfully in the hollow of my throat, I realized that John Lowndes might never have turned over that key to the owner of this house.

I was able to fold that paper and thrust it down the front of my jacket. Then I just stood there, knowing I had no time to run down those narrow stairs and seek a hiding place. A fraction of a second later I realized that

I at least could blow out the lamp. But as I took a step toward it, I saw a figure appear in the salon doorway.

I stared into the far reaches of the shadowy room, as if seeing a ghost. No, in this house and at this hour, the sudden appearance of a ghost would have been less bewildering to me.

He must have been surveying me, and the platform, and the wreckage on the floor, because after a moment he said, "The arsenal explosion? Yes, I suppose that is what we have to thank for this."

He made his way over the wreckage-strewn floor. I watched him, still too astonished to say anything at all, as he climbed the stairs. He stood there, a smile on his round and rosy face, and his glasses glittering in the lamplight. "You should have gone back to your concierge's flat, Martha, as I told you to."

I found my voice. "I saw John on the street. His face looked—awful. I ran from him, and hid in a doorway, and—"

"And eventually made your way here. Unfortunate."

Perhaps the night's events had clouded my wits. It was not until he said "Unfortunate" that I felt the first stir of fear.

He was looking at the wooden shield. "The two-headed ram. The emblem of the Crecys. Do you recall my talking at the Christmas Eve party about the Duke de Crecy? How it was said that for two years, while hiding in this house, he eluded capture? Yes, I think you must have been at the party by then. Perhaps it was your presence that reminded me of that story."

And earlier tonight at the ambulance, when in my confusion and fear I had told him of my mother's dying words, he had decided to search this house.

No, to search it again.

I said, from a throat that felt dry, "Where did you get that key?"

"Key? Oh, the one I used just now. A locksmith made it for me. I had plenty of time some months ago to make a wax impression of the lock."

Plenty of time, while I lay all night in that room at the ambulance, helplessly sick from whatever he had slipped into my wine.

"Did you find something behind that shield, Martha? A piece of paper, perhaps?"

"No."

He took the shield down from the wall. It had hung, I saw now, from a large square-headed nail, almost a spike, which had been driven into the stone wall. He reversed the shield and looked at its back. Turning it in his hands, he felt all around its edge. "One solid piece of wood."

He rehung the shield, and then turned back to me. "Give it to me, Martha."

"I don't know what you mean."

"You should not try to lie. You have the wrong sort of face for it."

I saw him reach into the pocket of his coat. Something gleamed briefly in the lamplight. Mother-of-pearl? Then it seemed to me that I could see nothing except the round mouth of the gun in his hand.

"It is a small pistol, what you Americans call a lady pistol, because it easily can be concealed—in a muff, say. It's ineffective at any great distance. But only a few feet separate us. Now hand it over, Martha."

Paralyzed, I stared at that little object in his hand. Even though I did not move, I felt that my body was shrinking in on itself, trying to escape the bullet that in another moment might smash into fragile flesh and bone.

"Where have you put it, Martha? You are carrying no reticule. At the ambulance I noticed that apparently you had dashed out of your flat without it." He paused. "Did you put that paper down the front of your jacket? Or perhaps in your skirt pocket?"

If he were about to kill me, why was he asking where I had put that folded piece of paper?

And then at last my numbed brain began to function, and I knew why. Blood soaking into that paper might make those numbers and symbols undecipherable. And so, until he knew where he could shoot safely, he would not shoot at all.

But he might try to rush at me and strike me over the head with the pearl handle of that little gun . . .

I took a sidewise step, moving closer to the platform's edge. Surely he would not risk rushing at me now, lest in our struggle we both plunge to the salon floor.

"Stand still, Martha."

I stood still. I said, past the pulse pounding in my throat, "First you must tell me what that paper is."

He seemed to consider. "All right. Perhaps when you know you will realize how very, very serious I am about this. There is an old chemist named Richard who worked for Baron Perruchot. He was trying to develop a new form of anesthetic. But when he used the vapor he had concocted on experimental animals, all of them died. Now do you see the value of his formula?"

I shook my head, remembering how Professor Richard had said, "It was a failure, a shocking failure."

"My dear child! Any government with such a vapor among its weapons would have an enormous advantage.

What if the French had been able to use it last winter? Balloons could have carried the vapor aloft in highly breakable glass canisters, and dropped them among the Prussian troops. Then it might have been Frenchmen marching through Berlin, not Prussians through Paris. Now do you understand?"

Yes, I understood.

I also understood that he did not intend to let me live, whether or not I handed over that paper. He could not afford to, now that I knew the terrible significance of those letters and symbols.

Monsieur Bitzius said, "The Baron saw the value of the formula, so he appropriated it, and asked the Professor to say nothing about it, which I imagine the poor old fool was glad to do."

But contrary to Monsieur Bitzius, the old man had not been entirely a fool. Later on, realization had struck him. Hysterical with fear of how—and by whom—his formula might be employed, he had tried to regain possession.

My lips felt wooden. "If it was kept secret, how is it that you heard—"

"My dear girl, there are no perfectly kept secrets. Always there are rumors—in this case, about a number of dead animals removed from the Perruchot laboratory. And in my business, one learns to pay attention to rumors."

His business. I knew what his business was, now. He had splendid camouflage for it. As that eternal neutral, a Swiss, he was able to travel more or less freely across the borders of even warring nations. He was a "financier," a term so vague that any man obviously well-supplied with money might call himself that. And his endowment of the ambulance had brought him quasi-official status and widespread respect, almost as much respect as it had brought to that English philanthropist, Richard Wallace.

An irrelevant thought intruded. There had been talk of naming a boulevard after Richard Wallace. Would there someday be a Rue Ferdinand Bitzius?

Ask questions, I ordered myself. As long as I could keep him answering . . .

"Did Philippe—did the Baron plan to sell the paper to the French government?"

"Louis Napoleon's government? Of course not. Like everyone else who could see a yard in front of his face, Perruchot knew that Louis Napoleon would soon be finished, and that the Prussians eventually would win the war. They were the customers he had in mind."

"And—and you?"

"I am strictly neutral. I sell for the best price I can get. And now that I have explained why I must have that paper, please hand it over, and then go home, or stay here, or do whatever you please, just as long as you tell no one about this. No one, do you understand? I hate to make threats, but if you do become loose-lipped, you'll pay for it."

He extended his left hand. "Now give it to me, like a good girl. I can't stand here the rest of the night pointing a gun at you."

Clever Monsieur Bitzius. But like many clever people, he had a weakness. He tended to regard others—perhaps especially a terrified young woman—as fools. Did he really think I could believe he would allow me to walk out of this house?

"Not—not yet," I said. "First you've got to tell me

about my mother. I have a right to know that, don't I?"

He said nothing, but I saw his face stiffen at mention of my mother. If any doubt had been in my mind for the last few minutes, it was gone now. His was the face, the friendly face of her daughter's employer, which she had seen when she parted the salon draperies that night.

I stretched my arm backward a little and grasped the carved bedpost, as if to steady myself. "Did the Baron leave instructions with my mother to sell that paper to Frederick Mosser?"

I saw surprise in the eyes behind the silver-rimmed spectacles. He had expected me to ask something else. "Yes, Mosser was to buy it on behalf of the Prussians. But he was a cautious man, Mosser. Apparently he wanted to wait until the Prussians occupied Paris, so that the transaction would be safer. But they did not occupy it. They merely marched through. And now, of course, he is out of the picture."

When I said nothing, just looked at him questioningly, he added, "Didn't you know? The Versailles shelling has killed a number of people in Passy these last few weeks. Frederick Mosser was one of them. All right, Martha. I've waited long—"

"No!" My voice was shrill. "I have a right to know more about my mother. Did—did she know what that formula was?" Even with fear of that gun filling my consciousness, I still had room to hope that she had not known.

"The Baron had told her it was a new type of gunpowder. Otherwise all she knew was that it represented money, and that the Baron had said Mosser would pay the most money. A very single-minded woman, your mother. She admitted possession of the formula, but refused to even bargain with me until she had seen Mosser. I saw how lacking she was in any sort of judgment. Now that she knew that someone beside herself and Mosser knew of the formula's existence, she might have become panicky after I left, and gone to the police. So I did what I had to do."

What he had to do. Hoping to kill her swiftly and silently, without arousing the rest of the household, he had used that paper knife, and then walked out of the house.

"You see, Martha, even though you had not asked that question, I have answered it. I want you to realize that I will not hesitate to use violence if you force me to. But I don't want to hurt you. I never have."

"You hurt me the night you hit me over the head."

Again he looked startled, as if he found that conversational leap disconcerting. "That was unfortunate. I had come here to look in the most obvious place—the safe. Since knowing how to open safes is part of my business, I would have been able to look through it even if I had found it locked. But I did not. When I found nothing inside it to interest me, I was ready to leave. Unfortunately, I knocked over that bit of statuary. I was afraid that you or your mother might have been awakened, and might look out the window and see me crossing the courtyard. And so I just waited. When you came into the salon, I had to hit you over the head—with the handle of the gun I have in my hand right now."

The gun. I stared at that ugly little muzzle, and then forced my gaze upward to his face. "You bribed our housekeeper to leave the door open for you that night, didn't you?"

He spoke with weary impatience. "No, I merely ordered her to. She is an employee of mine. I find it useful to seek out people like her—ones who can be controlled with both the carrot and the stick."

"The carrot and—"

"The carrot is the small retainer I pay her. The stick is the threat to tell the police her real name. I have no intention of telling you her life story, much as you would like me to. Suffice it to say that if she had not escaped from a Marseilles prison a few years ago, she would now be serving a life sentence at the penal colony in Numea."

I thought of Madame Duchamps' cold, sly face. "The couple who used to work for Philippe and my mother. Did you know the restaurant owner who—"

"Of course. He owed me a few favors. Besides, he needed a good chef. Once the position here was open, I sent Madame Duchamps to apply." He smiled. "Philippe Perruchot never could resist a bargain."

He paused and then went on rapidly, as if to forestall further questions, "When I came back here Christmas Eve, of course, there was no one to leave the place unlocked, and so I had to break the basement window. And now, Martha, if there is nothing else you want to know—"

Frantically I searched my mind for something else to say, anything at all. "That formula doesn't belong to you!" The words were childish, I knew, but perhaps they would win me a few more precious seconds. "It belongs to Philippe!"

His expression was quizzical. "So you know he's alive. Lowndes picked up that story, I suppose, when he was out of Paris last fall. Well, since he hasn't had the courage to come back to Paris for that paper you're hiding, it belongs to whoever can get it. Now hand it over, Martha."

I could think of nothing more to say. As we looked at each other through the lamplight, I saw resolution gathering in his face. His patience, like my brain, was exhausted. He would risk using force.

"Please," I said, "please." Tightening my grip on the bedpost, I took a cautious step backward. Only about eighteen inches of platform separated the outward edge of the bed from that sheer drop. If I could retreat to that narrow space, he might not dare to struggle with me. And if he fired, perhaps the bedpost . . .

"Stop right there, Martha."

I froze. The gun in his hand no longer pointed at my body, but at my forehead.

From the corner of my eye I saw movement, over there in the shadowy reaches of the salon. I turned my head. Someone stood in the doorway. Now he had moved forward into the room . . .

"Watch out!" I screamed. "He's got a gun."

Monsieur Bitzius did not turn his head. "Martha! Such an ancient device. Now this is your last . . ."

And then he, like me, must have heard the running footsteps, because he whirled around. He fired once, and then, as the crouching figure kept moving forward, fired again.

Perhaps I made some movement, although I do not recall doing so. All I know is that Monsieur Bitzius whirled toward me, his round face white now and set in a grimace that made him almost unrecognizable.

"Get down!" John shouted.

As I threw myself across the foot of the bed, I heard

the gun's report. And then I not only felt, but heard, the ancient bed's collapse, the splintering of its wood, the rending sound as the bedposts at the foot toppled.

I did not see him throw up his arms to protect himself from a falling post, nor did I see him lose his balance on the platform's edge. But I did hear his cry as he plunged.

I lay there, unable to move. In my nostrils was a strange smell—dust, worm-eaten wood, rotting fabric. I thought, with weird irrelevance, "The smell of centuries."

Chapter 25

Footsteps swiftly climbing the stairs. John said, "Don't move. You may bring down those posts at the head of the bed. Are you all right?"

I raised heavy eyelids and saw him standing there on the platform between those two fallen bedposts. "Yes."

"Don't move," he said again. "Wait here. I have to find out . . ."

Seconds later I heard scraping sounds, and knew he was moving some of the wrecked paneling about. For perhaps a minute there was silence. Then I heard him cross to one of the salon windows. A ripping sound. He must have pulled down one of those gold brocade draperies. He recrossed the salon, and again moved some of the paneling about.

I heard him climbing the stairs. "Just lie still for a moment more. I'm going to hold up those other two posts." I heard him move along that narrow space between the bed's edge and that sheer drop. He stepped over my extended legs.

"All right. Better not risk standing up at the side of the bed. Can you swing your body around and slide off at the foot?"

"Yes."

A moment later I got to my feet and stood there swaying. He came swiftly along that narrow space. He picked up the lamp in one hand and, his other hand holding mine, moved ahead of me down the stairs.

"Over there, on that sofa between the windows." A small table stood beside the sofa. He placed the lamp on it.

We sat down. I could not see the figure he must have covered with the drapery. "Is he—"

"Yes, a broken neck. I arranged some of that paneling so you wouldn't have to . . ." He broke off, and then asked, "Can you talk about it?"

"Not just yet. Give me a little time."

"All right."

After a moment I asked, "How did you get in here? The basement window?"

"Yes. I saw the broken pane. That made me almost sure you were in this house."

Again I was silent. Then I said, "When I saw you on the street tonight, I thought—"

"I know what you thought, or at least some of it. It was in your face."

"I'd found those letters and that picture of Laura Hathaway." Beneath my leaden exhaustion, I felt a stir of the rage which had shaken me as I read those letters.

"I know. When the concierge told me how you had rushed out, giving no reason, I asked her if you'd had a caller. I thought that was what might have upset you. She said no one but you had been upstairs."

I said, in a voice that sounded toneless to my own ears, "And then you thought of that box on the wardrobe shelf."

209

"Yes. I could tell you had been into it. I remembered putting the photograph on the bottom, face down, with the letters on top of it."

I said, with an effort, "Are you in love with her?"

"No. How can you even ask that? I thought I might be, once, but . . ."

He broke off and then said, "Will you let me try to explain it?" When I did not answer, he went on, "I felt that Laura and James had given me an opportunity to prevent a great injustice to two friends I was fond of. Also, there was your grandmother. I liked her. I hated the thought of her credulity being imposed upon.

"And they were so plausible, those two. Before I left New York, they had me quite convinced that your mother was thoroughly dissolute, and had been even while her husband was alive. I thought that they had first-hand knowledge of her adulteries. It was only good breeding, I thought, that kept them from giving me the details."

My voice shook. "Including the name of one certain lover, I suppose—the one whose daughter she had palmed off as—"

"Yes. But wait, Martha. Please wait. They had showed me no pictures of your father. They never actually said that he had been as blond as they are, and as your mother was, any more than they actually said so in the letter you read. But the implication was there."

Yes, the implication had been in the letters. John only would have to "look" at me, those letters had said, to know I could not possibly be a Hathaway. But he had done more than look.

"Why did you come to our theater box that night?"

"I suppose because something about their letters—

Laura's insistence that I not talk to either of you, for instance—had raised a shadowy doubt in my mind. And when, about ten days later, you showed me that locket with Charles Hathaway's picture in it, and I saw how much you looked like him—well, the whole thing fell apart. That night I sent them a letter saying, in effect, that I knew how they had tried to use me, and that I wanted no more correspondence with either of them. I also told them that I had written a letter to your grandmother's lawyer, telling what they'd tried to do, and advising that he show your grandmother my letter unless those two stopped bullying her about her will."

He paused, and then went on, "I intended to send her photograph back to Laura, and her letter and her brother's. There was a certain amount of vengefulness in that. I could imagine their faces burning as they read their own sly, sanctimonious letters. But by the time I actually got around to sending them back, it was too late. Paris was under siege. And all that was going out by balloon were government communications and the briefest of personal missives. True, I could have taken that box with me when I passed through the Prussian lines for the *Observer*. But the Prussians, even though they were polite about it, gave every document in the possession of journalists a thorough inspection. I felt so rotten about my own part in the whole thing that I hated the thought of anyone else reading those letters."

"And so you put it up on the wardrobe shelf."

"Yes. I intended to send it to them when the siege was lifted. But by that time so much had happened that—well, I simply forgot about that box. Maybe I wanted to."

I said, into the silence, "But you couldn't forget why you had approached us that night at the theater."

"No, nor why I took you driving in the Bois that afternoon. I was certain you would despise me if you knew. That was why I stayed away from you, even after we went through that marriage ceremony. I couldn't face the look I would see in your eyes when I told you."

Yes, even after the marriage ceremony he had stayed away from me. It was not until I had thrown myself into his arms . . .

He said, as if his thoughts had followed mine, "What we've had for such a little while has been so wonderful, Martha. I couldn't bring myself to risk ruining it, not just yet."

I said, from a constricted throat, "You were afraid of what you would see in my face if I knew." I turned toward him. "Well, I know now. Look in my face."

He looked for perhaps three seconds. Then he reached out for me. It was far from being our first kiss. And yet as he held me in his arms, his lips warm upon mine, I felt it was more meaningful than all our kisses in the past, even the first one.

Moments later, as I sat with my head against his shoulder, I reflected that it was now I who had something to hide. Perhaps I would never tell him, or at least not for a long time, that I thought he might have been the one my mother had admitted to this room that night.

I said, "What made you realize I might be here?"

"I didn't, at first. I just thought you might try to get to safe territory, where the fighting had stopped. So I kept working my way toward the river. When I reached the quay in front of the Louvre, I turned left. It's good that I did. A fireman at the Hôtel de Ville told me that a girl of your description had crossed the bridge. I was almost certain then where you had gone."

We were silent for a few moments. I became aware that the first gray light had entered the undraped window behind us. So it was over, this night that had seemed endless. And then, unbelievably, the blackbird in the courtyard tree sounded its first sleepy notes. Here in this ravaged city, beneath a pall of smoke, a bird was singing.

"Can you talk now? About what happened here tonight?"

I told him, sharply aware of the motionless figure he had hidden from my view. When I had finished, I said, "What I can't understand is how my mother—"

"The Baron had told her it was some new sort of gunpowder. Don't you see? Men have been killing each other with guns for more than three hundred years. What difference to her if they use another sort of powder?"

"Still, to—to hope to make money out of—"

"I know, I know. But some people feel very hard-pressed. To them, certain moral scruples seem more than they can afford."

Yes, she had felt hard-pressed indeed. She was forty, and the Baron was dead, and she had almost no money. Perhaps it was little wonder she had been tempted to make all that she could from that formula, a formula more hellish than she could have guessed.

I reached down the front of my jacket. When I had unfolded the paper, I leaned across the sofa arm and held it above the lamp chimney. I heard John's exclamation, but he made no move to stop me. The paper turned brown. When it burst into flames, I dropped it at my feet, waited a few seconds, and then ground it into blackened powder under the sole of my shoe.

"That's the end of it," I said.

"Oh, my poor darling." When I looked at him, puzzled, he said, "Don't you know that sooner or later, whatever weapon the human mind can conceive of will be . . ." He broke off. "But maybe I'm wrong." He got up, blew out the lamp, and then sat down beside me again. "We had better go soon."

"In a few minutes. John, I can't hear gunfire."

"Maybe the wind is in the wrong direction. Or maybe it's all over. It's bound to be soon. There can't be more than a couple of hundred Communards left. They don't have a chance. Maybe they never did."

I turned my head on his shoulder and buried my face in his neck. "Why must the world be so terrible?"

"I don't know. It isn't always. And even at the worst times—well, listen to that bird out there! Maybe it knows something we don't. Maybe there's hope for the world, as long as a bird can still sing."

And as long as two people could love each other. Love enough to keep running forward, as John had, despite the bullets spitting from that gun.

"Shall we try to get home now? And later, we'll really go home. While I was looking for you last night, I made up my mind to that. I'm going to ask the *Observer* to transfer me back to New York as soon as possible."

He stood up and held out his hands to clasp mine. "Come on, darling. Let's go."

As we went out through the courtyard, the blackbird was still singing.